Praise for *The Brutal Language of Love*

"Very much in the footsteps of Mary [...] group of tales that are lip-biters, intent[...]
—*The Hartford Courant*

"There is a certain amount of guilty pleasure involved in reading this debut collection, because Alicia Erian regularly commits infractions against the Etiquette of the Short Story. . . . In [her] tenderest works, . . . Erian earns her title. . . . Sex is less a teleology than an alphabet, composing endless possibilities."
—*The Village Voice*

"Alicia Erian's stories sneak up on you. The calm, direct, quietly self-effacing, and remarkably unflinching voice of these narratives is always telling a more complicated story than it appears to be. The reveals are so subtle and well crafted that the reader feels rich and rewarded every single time."
—Pam Houston, author of *Cowboys Are My Weakness*

"[Erian's] stories are so propulsive that I couldn't resist her hapless heroines."
—*Mademoiselle*

"Seductive, erotic, smart and tartly humorous, these tales are true gems."
—*Publishers Weekly* (starred review)

"*The Brutal Language of Love* is a jumble of contradictions—silly and smart, truthful and ridiculous, heartless and suddenly, painfully heartfelt. Alicia Erian is an original, and very funny, too."
—Mary Gaitskill, author of *Because They Wanted To*

"[Erian is] good at capturing the dark and sensual underside of life. [But] she cares, and it comes across."
—*Library Journal*

"Erian presents her world in hilarious, unsentimental prose."
—*Entertainment Weekly*

"In Alicia Erian's provocative debut collection, young women go looking for love and find only trouble, around the world and across the street. *The Brutal Language of Love* maps out a dark landscape of risk and desire, illuminated by vivid flashes of humor and insight."
—Tom Perotta, author of *Election*

The Brutal Language
of Love

Alicia Erian

The Brutal Language of Love

stories

Simon & Schuster Paperbacks

New York   London   Toronto   Sydney

Simon & Schuster Paperbacks
A Division of Simon & Schuster, Inc.
1230 Avenue of the Americas
New York, NY 10020

Copyright © 2001 by Alicia Erian
Originally published in hardcover by Random House, Inc.

Acknowledgment is made to the publications in which these stories first appeared: "Bikini" in *The Sun;* "Standing Up to the Superpowers" in *Confrontation;* "Almonds and Cherries" in *The Iowa Review;* "Lass" in *Zoetrope;* "When Animals Attack" in *The Barcelona Review;* "Alcatraz" in *Nerve.*

First Simon & Schuster trade paperback edition July 2008

SIMON & SCHUSTER PAPERBACKS and colophon are registered trademarks of Simon & Schuster, Inc.

For information about special discounts for bulk purchases, please contact Simon & Schuster Special Sales at 1-800-456-6798 or business@simonandschuster.com.

Manufactured in the United States of America

10 9 8 7 6 5 4 3 2 1

Library of Congress Cataloging-in-Publication Data
Erian, Alicia.
  The brutal language of love : stories / Alicia Erian.
    p. cm.
1. Love stories, American. 2. Young women—Fiction. I. Title.
PS3555.R4265B78 2001
813'.6—dc21

ISBN-13: 978-1-4165-9271-6
ISBN-10:   1-4165-9271-7 .

for David Franklin

Contents

The Brutal Language
of Love

Standing Up to the Superpowers

Beatrice told Shipley she would sleep with him, and then she passed out. When she awoke the next morning, he said he'd gone ahead without her. He got dressed and asked her to drive him to the police station so he could turn himself in for rape, but she said not to worry about it. She wasn't happy, she said, but it was her own fault for drinking with a freshman. Shipley walked to the police station and turned himself in anyway. A Lieutenant Verbena called to see if Beatrice wanted to press charges and she said no. "Put him on," Beatrice said, and when Shipley said hello she hung up.

He called her the next day to say his mother, a pediatrician, had suggested she take a morning-after pill. "You told your mother?" Beatrice asked.

"She's a doctor," Shipley said.

"I got that."

"I'm going into counseling for my drinking," he added.

"How old are you?"

"Eighteen."

"I'm twenty-two," she said. "Now leave me alone."

Beatrice was a junior. She had taken a year off from college to work in a cheap clothing store for older women, then returned to school when she realized she made more money living off student loans. Her father, a divorce lawyer who had successfully represented himself against Beatrice's mother, had promised to help with tuition as long as Beatrice did well in high school. When she turned out to be not quite as smart as early test scores had indicated, however, he reneged. His advice to her was to stay away from the humanities, where there were no jobs.

She signed up for a Russian literature course with a professor named Fetko, who gave her good marks for implying that she'd be willing to sleep with him. Sometimes in his office he'd let her sip from his vending machine coffee, or take bites from the sandwiches his wife had prepared for him. Other times he gave her quarters for her own snacks. Mostly they just sat around shooting the shit, talking about Chekhov and his famous hemorrhoids.

Shipley, the freshman, was also in Russian literature. Fetko hated him and so did Beatrice. He was always asking stupid questions and interrupting Fetko's flow, something that was very important to Fetko. "Get him drunk and fuck with his head," Fetko had instructed Beatrice. "That would be worth a letter grade to me." Now, as she sat before her professor after Monday's class, Beatrice was unsure of what to say. "I fucked with him," she began, but when she described exactly how, Fetko turned white. "Jesus, Beatrice," he said, letting his pipe hang limp from his mouth.

She shrugged. She had been asleep when it happened.

Shipley called that afternoon to ask about the morning-after pill. Beatrice was sitting in her attic bedroom in a house filled with students. She had slept with two film majors on the second floor, one of whom had gone to great lengths to explain his uncircumcised penis to her. This had made her laugh—something she rarely did—and lose all interest in him, though she let him screw her anyway. "You're so hot," he'd whispered in her ear. "All the guys in the house want you."

"Thanks," she'd said, waiting for him to finish. Compliments had stopped doing it for her a long time ago.

Today she was trying to read a book about China for a history class. The professor was old and deaf, and whenever she tried to make a pass at him, he'd bellow, "What?" It was a grade she would actually have to work for, and it was killing her. Sometimes she went to his office to tell him this and he just nodded, pretending he could hear. She was no dummy. Her brain had just stopped accepting academic text along with the compliments.

What kind of name was Shipley anyway? Beatrice had

half a mind to ask him now that he was on the phone, but didn't like to encourage friendship. Anyway, she was irritated, sick of his mother and this morning-after crap. "Don't worry about it," she told him. "I'm on birth control."

"What kind?" he asked, panting a little.

"What do you mean what kind?"

"What brand?"

"I don't know."

"Generic is cheaper."

"Fuck off."

He laughed. "You have a nice personality. I liked you even before we got drunk."

"Thanks."

"You wanna keep talking?"

"Let me think. No."

"I tried to talk to you after class today but you left so fast I couldn't find you."

"Try to breathe slower," Beatrice instructed him.

"Can I talk to you after class on Wednesday?"

"No."

"Before class?"

She hung up on him. He was in love with her, that much was clear. It happened all the time; men loved her personality, thought it was nice. Not nice-nice obviously, but nice-honest. Back home, people said she was like her mother, who was often described as acidic, and who had become a lesbian after Beatrice left for college. "Sex is sex," she had once advised her daughter. "No need to be picky." What bothered Beatrice was her mother's refusal to come out in the liberal, northwestern city where she lived, instead preferring to divulge the intimate details of her love life solely to Beatrice, over the telephone.

"I don't want to hear it, Mom," Beatrice would say, at which point her mother would accuse her of being homophobic. Beatrice protested, saying she had never felt comfortable with her mother's bedroom stories about her father either. "So I guess I'll kill myself," was her mother's response, "if my own daughter won't even talk to me." It was Beatrice's freshman year and she didn't need the responsibility, so she listened. She allowed herself to be lost track of as a sophomore, however, moving off-campus and delisting her number. There was some comfort in knowing that neither of her parents had ever been of a mind to chase after her.

Increasingly, Beatrice loved no one. She had a fair amount of sex but in general preferred her own company, and on occasion that of Fetko. He had information about dead writers that fascinated her, health problems and such. She told him that after he died, people would say he had liked for his girl students to talk dirty to him, but he said no one would care since he wasn't a real writer. She pointed out his books of criticism and he told her she was sweet to be so naïve, to have such big tits. In the end, though, she was glad he never tried to touch them, that it never went beyond talk. This would have weakened their rapport, which was something she felt they definitely enjoyed. Everybody traded on what they had, after all, and if what you had wasn't pretty, well, there was still a friend for you.

IN class on Wednesday, Fetko seemed distracted. When Shipley raised his hand and asked him to expand upon the socioeconomic conditions of the lady with the pet dog, he did so without protest. Later, when Beatrice went to meet him in his office, he wasn't there. A note on his door said he was ill and that office hours had been canceled. Beatrice hoped Fetko's guilt over what had happened between her and Shipley would not jeopardize their arrangement. She had enough on her plate worrying about China without the added anxiety of having to complete his assignments as well.

At a vending machine she purchased lunch—a chocolate bar and pretzels, neither of which would taste like anything, she already knew. She found a bench on a wide walkway in front of the tall Humanities Building, and looked down into the valley at the poor town she had sold ugly clothes to the previous year. It's better up here, she thought, though she knew she would tumble down the hill soon enough.

Moments later she was joined by Shipley, a fat, sweaty guy with a dumb haircut. People's appearances were of little concern to Beatrice. She bedded the handsome and the homely alike. Along with her taste buds had gone her sense of smell, and she didn't miss it. Sex, she believed, should be more of a democratic process, distributed only when a situation—and not a person—merited it.

He presented her with a card depicting Monet's *Water Lilies* and containing a message that read, *Sorry I raped you—Shipley.*

"It's not funny, you know," she said, thrusting the card back at him.

He took it. "I know."

"Then what the hell is that?" she said, motioning toward the card. He was picking at it with his wet fingers.

"My parents think I should try to make it up to you."

"Are you retarded or something?"

He laughed, relieved. "You have a *great* personality."

"You are retarded," she said.

"I'm in college," he offered.

"You have some sort of emotional retardation," she surmised, "some sort of freakishness in that way."

He shrugged. Suddenly, a strange concern that she had hurt his feelings came and went. "Well," she said, "I guess I'll take the card back."

He handed it to her, then sat down on the bench. Her nylon book bag lay between them, and she made no attempt to move it. "You're my first," he said.

"Is that right?" she said. She had been many, many firsts.

"That's why you're kind of special to me."

"Uh-huh." She was alternating: a bite of chocolate, a bite of pretzel. Sweet, salt, sweet, salt. It tasted like a little something.

"I'd like you to meet my parents," he said hopefully.

"You're a nice kid," she said. "I don't really like to meet people's parents."

"My mother feeds expired birth control pills to our plants," he said, "to fertilize them."

"Stop talking about that," she snapped.

"Sorry," he said.

They spent the rest of the afternoon like that: together, but not too close.

Felko seemed back to his normal self on Friday. He refused to acknowledge Shipley's request for an accounting of Babel's whereabouts on the eve of the revolution, and was in his office after class. But when Beatrice asked him softly what she would find if she unzipped his pants, he stared back at her blankly. "Beatrice," he said, rubbing his eyes, "I've made a mistake here. We can talk as much as you want—anytime you want—but not about the stuff we used to talk about. And you need to start doing better on your quizzes."

She left his office, stunned. She went home and masturbated, then fell asleep. A call from Shipley woke her at around eleven that night. "What do you want?" she demanded.

"I'm hoping we're going to make love again sometime soon. When you're awake."

"Forget it." She sat up in bed and noticed how perfectly her square, latticed windows framed an amoebic moon.

"What's the matter?" he asked.

"My boyfriend dumped me."

"You have a boyfriend?"

"Had."

"Wow." He paused for a moment before saying, "Well, that's great! Now I have a better chance!"

She laughed for the first time since the explanation of the uncircumcised penis. "I guess you do."

"Really?" he asked, excited.

She woke up a little more. "No."

She went on to tell him about China, as a sort of review for a test she had the next day. He listened intently, and she was surprised at a man more than satisfied by this kind of talk.

She failed the test, having spent too much time studying the health of the Chinese—acupuncture and such—as opposed to agriculture and commerce. She wasn't doing much better in Russian literature, where she had begun sitting next to Shipley and passing him questions intended to drive the professor mad. Upon receipt of these, Shipley would instantly raise his hand and ask, "Is *Lolita* a memoir?" or, "Have you ever been to the Russian circus?" Though Fetko eventually stopped calling on him, Shipley continued to wave his arm around maniacally, complaining frequently of numbness in his fingers. It was during this period that Beatrice first knew herself to giggle.

She could've scared Fetko, she knew—could've threatened to turn him in if he didn't keep her grades up. But the thought of this reminded her too much of that first night with Shipley: how, because she had set out to harm him, the whole thing was really all her fault. In reporting either man she would only incriminate herself—reveal that she was a fraud who would do anything to keep her good grades and student loans. There was no point. Her only recourse now was to brace herself, China and Russia having allied themselves against her.

Shipley had an old VW van he drove Beatrice around in after class. He bought her lunch with a credit card belonging to a Shipley Sr., and wrote stories in which the two of them met Chekhov and took him to the doctor. He let Beatrice stick a fine sewing needle in his face and insisted it made him feel better all around. Knowing her financial situation, he cut her envelopes of coupons, brought her bags of pharmaceutical samples from his mother's office. They lay side by side on the grassy campus hills, drinking children's cough syrup and chewing Flintstones vitamins until the sun set over the Fine Arts Building and they fell asleep, waking up with bugs and grass in their hair. The word *idyllic* sprang to Beatrice's mind more than once, but she ignored it, thinking it was probably just anxiety. For when she wasn't with Shipley, she was irritable, unsettled. She had lost track of some of her unhappiness and could not seem to relocate it, not even in the bedrooms of the boys on the second floor—though she had looked.

"Do you remember anything about my penis?" Shipley asked her on the hillside one evening. The pollen count had been high that day, and they were passing a bottle of nasal spray back and forth.

"Not really," Beatrice said.

"Wow," he said.

"Yup," she said. "Imagine that."

"Hey, why did your boyfriend dump you?"

"Why?"

Shipley nodded.

"He was jealous of you," Beatrice said.

"He knows me?"

"He's been watching us," she confirmed.

This silenced Shipley for some time. It was a Sunday during finals, and the campus was deserted. "Would you like to see my penis?" he asked.

She looked over at his crotch. "Is it anything special?"

"I think so," he said.

She nodded. He took it out. "Okay," she said. "I saw it."

"It doesn't ring a bell?"

"No." She passed him the nasal spray.

He inhaled deeply, pinching the side of his empty nostril. "If I left it out," he said, sniffling, "would you do anything with it?"

"Probably not."

"Because I raped you?"

"Probably."

He put it away. "My mother thinks you should go for counseling," he said as he zipped up his fly.

"Why?"

"She says I raped you and you need to face that reality."

"I already did," she said.

"You're supposed to get mad, though."

"I'm busy," she said. "Doesn't your mother know anger is unproductive?"

"Is there anything that would make you want to make love with me again?"

"Yes," she said.

"What is it?" he asked eagerly, but she said she didn't know.

She failed out of school and lost her student loans. They hired her back at the cheap clothing store, where she felt oddly invigorated by her co-workers' discussions of impostor perfumes and patio furniture. Shipley picked her up in the evenings in his VW van and drove her to the college, where they continued to lie on the grass and take medication. He told her if they got married people would give them money and small appliances. "I'm tired of trading," she said, and she fell asleep.

On a Tuesday in May, Fetko came into the clothing store with his wife. Summer was slow in retail, and so it was just Beatrice, her manager having stepped out for lunch. Fetko seemed startled to see her and immediately told his wife he didn't think she would find anything she liked here, but she told him to sit down in the chair by the dressing room and wait. "What do you know anyway?" she said, and so Fetko shuffled past Beatrice at the cash register, his eyes glued to the floor.

Beatrice watched him for a moment, thinking about how most male professors his age—maybe fifty—still dressed as if it were 1974. She thought how amazing it was that young, stylish women of the nineties managed to get crushes on them anyway, as if age and intelligence transcended fashion. She had never had a crush on Fetko, and suddenly regretted this. He was a depressed, inappropriate, badly dressed man, and all she had ever noticed was his grade book, his red pencil.

Beatrice approached his chair now, which was puce where it wasn't threadbare. "Can I offer you a magazine or something to drink, sir?" she asked. She had no magazine or drinks. It was a cheap store. But she was stirred by his grief and did not want it to end.

"No thanks," he said. Then he added, "Miss."

Beatrice nodded. "I'll just help your wife then," she said, and walked off.

Mrs. Fetko was stout and seemed drawn to a group of co-ordinating, boxy separates done up in feminine, floral prints. "May I say you have lovely skin, ma'am," Beatrice began, which was the truth. Mrs. Fetko laughed and reached into her purse for a business card. "Here's my secret, hon," she said, handing it to Beatrice. FULL BODY MASSAGE BY JULES, it read. "You can keep it," she added. "Now, what do you think about this?" She held up a pink-and-gray blouse and a matching gray skirt.

"Is there a special occasion?" Beatrice asked.

"My husband works up at the college and he was just awarded an endowed chair. Very impressive. So I need something to wear to the ceremony. How about this?" She had laid the pink group over her arm and was now into the teals.

Beatrice shrugged. "They're just the same exact things in different colors."

Mrs. Fetko laughed. "Tell it like it is! I love it. Here. Start a dressing room for me, babe."

Beatrice took the clothes from her and headed toward the back of the store, where Fetko was furiously examining a dry-cleaning receipt from his wallet. She put Mrs. Fetko's clothes in a cubicle and said, "Congratulations," when she came back out.

He looked up from his receipt blankly.

"On your award," Beatrice added.

"Thank you," he whispered.

"Do you remember me?" she asked.

"Of course I do," he hissed. "Please!"

"Just wondering," she said.

Mrs. Fetko tried on several outfits, none of which was any better or worse than the others. When she asked Fetko which one he liked best, he said he didn't know. She pressed him and he said, "The pink, okay?"

"Don't be such an ass, Fetko," she said, rolling her eyes at Beatrice before returning to the dressing room.

"What are *you* looking at?" Fetko asked Beatrice after his wife had gone.

"Nothing," she said.

He glanced at the dressing rooms, then back at Beatrice. "Say something good to me," he whispered, laying a hand across his groin. "Quick."

She said something. He closed his eyes and smiled a little, the way he used to do. "Say something else," he said, and she did.

In return he offered her nothing. There were no more grades left, no student loans. Furthermore, he had clearly come to understand that she wouldn't retaliate. She had never once complained about the D he had given her, never hinted she even *knew* of the trouble she could cause him. And now here he was, looking to gratify himself at her expense. Asking for a freebie. She had complied not out of fear or hopefulness, but rather gratitude, for at last she felt herself to be depleted, empty, and in need.

iN the vaN oN the way home she told Shipley she loved him. "Will we make love?" he asked hopefully.

"Probably not," she said. "It's not that kind of love."

"Oh," he said. "Well, maybe you could stop making love with everybody else."

"I'll think about it," she said.

"Really?" he asked.

"Sure."

They drove through town without saying much more. The old van heaved and lurched while Shipley coaxed it on for one more mile, up one more city hill. Beatrice noticed a woman at a bus stop wearing a dress from her store, and pointed this out to Shipley, who said she didn't look half bad from a distance. "My mother likes your store," he said. "She said she may come in this weekend."

Beatrice considered protesting but then remembered that the shop was a public place. "What does your mother look like?" she asked instead.

Shipley thought for a minute before saying, "My father," which was of no help whatever.

Later, on the way to the college, Beatrice felt herself wanting more to eat than just medicine, and mentioned as much to Shipley. They planned an elaborate evening of food and drink, then stopped off for ice cream before dinner. It was very wrong of them, and it tasted very good.

Alcatraz

My mother promised to take me shopping after the car was fixed, so that was how I found myself sitting next to her at the mechanic's that morning, reading over her shoulder as she wrote a letter to my Aunt Mitzy saying I was still fat. "Hey, you can't write that!" I said, pointing to the sentence about me with an orange fingertip. We were sitting in the small office beside the garage, where people popped in to pay for gas or buy themselves a snack for the road. I had just eaten two bags of Chee-tos myself and was considering a third when I saw my name in my mother's fine hand.

"Oh," my mother said, acting as if she hadn't just written it. "You're right, Roz." She began crossing it out and her face turned red. She was pretty embarrassed, which shocked me, since I figured she would turn the tables on me and say something like "Well! You shouldn't have been reading a private letter over my shoulder!" Even though I knew she would go home and finish it later (rewriting the crossed-out part and telling Aunt Mitzy how touchy I had gotten about it), I felt kind of powerful. When we went clothes shopping that afternoon, I hardly noticed I was the only thirteen-year-old in the misses department flipping through the size sixteen rack.

We got home before dinner, so I put on my snow clothes and crossed Hermitage Road, where they were putting up a new development—one much nicer than ours. Several foundations had already been dug and were now half-filled with snow, while a forklift sat abandoned in an empty lot. There were cement blocks piled up all over the place, metal barrels filled with construction trash, and a short row of Porta Pottis. The door to one was open and inside I found a picture of a half-naked woman in a skimpy Santa Claus outfit taped to the wall. I took it down and put it in my pocket for Jennings, who was at his grandmother's for the weekend.

It was hard work running around in the snow. Each time I hopped down into one of the foundations, it took me forever to pull myself back out again. I saw this as a challenge—another way to burn more calories, which was why I was out there in the first place. When I got home and the scale said I had only lost a pound, I thought it should have been more.

Mom and I ate spaghetti with Ragú for dinner. We usually made that or Old El Paso tacos, or else we went to

McDonald's. We had eaten more natural foods when Jonquil was still living with us since she liked to cook, but now that she was gone Mom said it was crazy to go to that kind of trouble for just two people. Mom said it was on Jonquil's head that I had gotten so damn fat, and she hoped my sister could live with that.

After dinner Mom left to spend the night with her beau, a retired army sergeant who felt that any of the four branches of the military would serve to set Jonquil straight. I had a job baby-sitting for the two Hermann boys. We made a deal that I would let them stay up as late as they wanted as long as they didn't tell on me for smoking their parents' cigarette butts. Once the boys had fallen asleep in front of the TV, I carried them upstairs, put them to bed, and called my sister.

My mother had kicked her out the year before for becoming unruly. Jonquil, who had been seventeen at the time, moved in with her boyfriend, Vic, and got pregnant. She and Vic made plans to marry but then Jonquil had a miscarriage and they called the wedding off. The family was relieved, which so infuriated Jonquil (since she had suffered such pain), that she put the wedding back on again. Her bridal gown was her senior prom dress, while Vic, who was reedy and slack-jawed, borrowed one of his father's suits. I cried like a fool at the ceremony because now I knew there was no chance in hell Jonquil was ever coming back to us. Aunt Mitzy and my mother told me not to worry—that Vic was an inbred and it wouldn't last—and for once I was glad about how nasty they got when they were together.

Jonquil knew everything about sex and she taught it to me. She said she didn't want me to end up marrying a screwball like Vic just to prove a point, like she had. She said this right in front of him, on the weekends when I went to stay with them in their apartment, and he just laughed like she was telling a joke. He kissed her, too, and I watched as both their mouths opened and their tongues came out, all rude and wet. I could watch them kiss for hours and, in fact, sometimes that was what ended up happening.

But Jonquil wasn't kidding, and what I knew that Vic didn't was that she was going to leave him as soon as she saved up enough money. He was pursuing an art degree at a community college, which Jonquil described as "double jeopardy." Meanwhile, she supported both of them on her receptionist's salary from Dr. Flay, the TV hypnotist. He didn't perform on TV but he ran a lot of ads describing how he could stop people from smoking, overeating, or a combination of the two. He was a blond, handsome man, and sometimes, my sister told me, spoke to his clients in a made-up foreign accent. As an employee, Jonquil was entitled to a 50 percent discount on his services, and since he liked her so much (feeling her natural thinness made him look like a success), he extended that privilege to her family and friends. I had saved up some baby-sitting money, so when I called Jonquil that night from the Hermanns' house, it was to ask her to make me an appointment.

"What for?" she said.

"Because," I said. "Mom wrote and told Aunt Mitzy I was fat."

Jonquil made a light blowing sound.

"Are you smoking again?" I asked her.

"Uh-huh."

"But I thought Dr. Flay cured you."

"He did," Jonquil said. "I just forgot to say the key word before I went to the grocery store and it screwed me up. I bought a pack."

"Oh."

"Anyway," Jonquil said, "when I was your age, Mom wrote and told Aunt Mitzy I was a tramp, so don't worry about it."

"Why?"

"Huh?"

"Why did she say you were a tramp?"

"Don't be such a dumb ass, Roz."

"Sorry," I said. I blew smoke from one of Mrs. Hermann's cigarette butts. I could tell it was hers from the purple lipstick on the filter tip.

"What's that noise?" Jonquil asked me.

"Nothing. I was just sighing."

Eventually she gave in and made me an appointment for that week. I sat in a dentist's chair while Dr. Flay indeed spoke softly in an accent that reminded me of Count Dracula. He dimmed the lights and projected a small red dot on the white wall in front of me, which I was to focus on intently. Meanwhile Dr. Flay stood behind me, massaging my temples and telling me I was getting sleepy, even though I wasn't. I felt bad for him that he was doing such a terrible job, so I played along, making my eyelids bob up and down when he came around front to see how I was doing. *"Thaht's eet,"* he said. *"Thaht's eet."*

With my eyes now closed, Dr. Flay spoke frankly to me about the state of my body, saying I had three rolls of fat on my stomach, and wouldn't it be nicer to have just one? He said I had a pretty face, like my sister's, but that a double chin on a seventh grader was nothing short of heinous. He noted that my thighs squashed together so tightly as to be prohibitive, which I didn't understand, and then asked me point-blank how I thought I would ever get a boyfriend. I wanted to bring up Jennings then, but I was supposed to be hypnotized and so kept my mouth shut. It alarmed me somewhat that Dr. Flay's voice was getting closer and closer, so I took a quick peek. He stood directly in front of me with his hand on his groin. I shut my eyes immediately but it was too late; he had seen me. He dropped his accent, gave me my key word (which would remind me of our session and instantly decrease my appetite), and snapped his fingers. I assumed this meant I could open my eyes, and I did. Dr. Flay wished me luck and gave me a bill for fifty dollars, to be paid in cash to my sister.

On the way home Jonquil and I stopped at a Wendy's drive-thru. I said *hiccup* and she said *lizard,* and we neither overate nor smoked. "Do you think I'll really get thin?" I asked her as we sat in the parking lot, eating our baked potatoes. Jonquil didn't want to eat in the dining room because it was nonsmoking and if her key word hadn't worked, she would have been screwed.

A section of her long brown hair dipped into her potato,

and she tucked it behind her ear, sucking the nonfat sour cream from the ends. "It's hard to say," she said. "The data are inconclusive."

Jonquil dropped me off at the end of my driveway, then spun her tires on the ice for a couple of seconds, trying to peel out. When I got inside, my mother said my sister had no manners, coming and going like that without so much as a hello, and demanded I agree with her on this point. I did so reluctantly, after which she further demanded my key word. I lied and said it was *Sputnik,* which we had just learned about that day in social studies. She had taco meat for Old El Paso simmering on the stove and asked suspiciously if I was hungry. I said no and she beamed. It was nice, being able to make her happy for once, so I didn't bother mentioning Wendy's.

I finished my homework quickly, then ran across the street to see Jennings, whose bedroom light was on. His mother, a handsome divorcee who wore high heels and a small brunette hairpiece at the crown of her head, answered the door. "Well," she said, "don't you have pink cheeks! The cold agrees with you, Roslyn." She told me Jennings was in his room and to go on up. I think she thought we couldn't possibly be making love since I was so overweight and Jennings was sort of handsome, but we were.

We had been making love since a few months before, when I had beaten Jennings at the spelling bee. I was the best speller in school, while Jennings was second best, and when I got ejected early for misspelling *quietus,* I could tell he thought he had the whole thing wrapped up. After losing, however, I went to the library to see what the word meant, and found the main pronunciation to be qui-*ee*-tus, not qui-*ay*-tus, as Mrs. Googan had said. My face burned with injustice. Had she not been so obscure I would never have spelled it Q-U-I-A-T-U-S, and, furthermore, would still be in the running. I lugged the dictionary back to the classroom to plead my case.

Mrs. Googan was shocked and appalled. Frankly, so was I. Jennings had a lot of friends—mean friends, who were already deeply offended by my weight. It wasn't like spoiling Jennings's chance to win the bee was going to make them treat me any better. At the same time, I wasn't sure things could get all that much worse.

In the end, Mrs. Googan allowed me back into the competition and I won. After school that day, I went across the street to apologize to Jennings, for what it was worth. He lay on his bed, inconsolable. I waited for him to kick me out of his room or call me fat ass or something, but he didn't. I went over to his bed and put my arm around him, and was momentarily surprised at how easy it was to get close to a popular person. Of course, Jennings and I had grown up together, so even though he was more popular than I was at school, there was a different hierarchy in the neighborhood. All the kids I baby-sat for adored me, and even though they were several years younger, the sheer volume of them conferred upon me a vague status of local, albeit fat, hero. Jennings knew this. He could call me names and play mean tricks on me at school all he wanted, but in the neighborhood we were nearly equals.

I had spent the weekend preceding the spelling bee with Jonquil and Vic, studying the dictionary and learning what an orgasm was, and all the ways a woman could get one, if she was lucky. "Jennings," I said that day in his room, "would you like to make love?" He stopped sniffling so much and said yes. I might not have offered except I believed his secondary sex characteristics had come in over the summer, and Jonquil told me when this happened, boys weren't so little and slippery inside you anymore.

After we had done it, Jennings thanked me and said he'd like to do it again soon. Having experienced my first orgasm with the minimum of effort, I agreed. Mostly we did it after school, before his mother got home. Then it didn't matter how noisy we were, or how long it took, or how often we wanted to do it. Through all of this, Jennings started to become a different person. In school, he was crueler to me than ever before, or so it seemed. We staged scenes where he shoved me against lockers for being so fat, then caught me just before I hurt myself and banged his own fist against the metal, so it just sounded bad. He grabbed me in front of his friends and whispered threats in my ear, which were really words of love such as, *I can't wait to see you this afternoon.* When we were alone, he told me he wanted to be a stunt coordinator when he grew up, so this was all just practice for him. He assured me constantly that my main problem was not so much that I was fat, but that I smelled bad, which I appreciated, since at least I could do something about that.

Now, standing in his doorway after returning from Dr.

Flay's office, I announced, "Jennings, I've been hypnotized."
He was lying on his side in bed, looking at *Playboy*. He set the
magazine aside and I could see he had an erection inside his
pants. He patted the bed for me to sit down beside him, and I
did. "I think I got ripped off," I said, even though I hadn't
overeaten at Wendy's.

"Why?" Jennings asked. He rolled over on his back so
that his erection pitched a tent inside his khakis. That was
what he called it.

"Because," I said. Absently, I put a hand on his crotch. "I
didn't feel weird or anything. I didn't feel dizzy."

"Did you black out?" Jennings asked me.

I shook my head. "No."

"What stinks?" he said.

I smelled under my arm. "Me."

"How about I give you a bath?" Jennings asked, turning
to look at me. He laid a hand over mine, which was still on
his crotch.

"With your mother downstairs?"

He shrugged. "She's leaving in a few minutes."

"Okay," I said. We waited until we heard the front door
slam then went into the bathroom. It wasn't the first bath Jennings had given me. He liked to wash between my legs then
get in with me and do it underwater. Sometimes we fell asleep
in the tub afterward. My mother always said I smelled good
when I came back from Jennings's, and I told her it was Ms.
Jennings's air freshener.

Before I left that evening I gave Jennings the picture of the lady Santa from the Porta Potti. He told me it was beautiful and that she looked just like me.

Jennings helped me study for the next round of the spelling bee, a citywide competition. For every ten words I got right, he touched me between my legs; for every ten words I got wrong, I sucked him off, which was no kind of punishment, really, since I enjoyed being intimate with Jennings.

In school he was getting tired of pretending he didn't like me, and sometimes, accidentally, he'd smile and wave when we passed each other in the hall. I wished he wouldn't do that since it only further infuriated his friends, who were still fuming over the way I had insinuated myself back into the spelling bee. They couldn't understand why Jennings wasn't angrier with me, and as far as I could tell, he had made them no explanations.

His friend Garrett was particularly mad. Garrett had the face of a desperate baby bird, framed by long yellow hair that he constantly shook out of his eyes instead of pushing back with his hands. His legs were bowed and he wore aviator glasses, just like my brother-in-law, Vic. It seemed unfair that I should be attacked for being fat when someone like Garrett was running around free, but that was the way it went.

Garrett sat behind me in music class and kicked me hard in the behind while we listened to Beethoven's Fifth, trying to decipher the cello parts. I kept waiting for Mrs. Krieg to hear the sound of my chair squawking across the floor, which it did every time Garrett's foot landed on my ass, but he was careful to kick me only when the music got loud. What could I do? He had two friends sitting on either side of him, laughing each time he made his move. My neck began to hurt more than my butt from the whiplash of being jerked around. I reached back to rub it and Garrett stabbed me in the finger with his pencil.

One afternoon when Jennings washed me, he said I had a yellow-and-blue bruise on my backside. I told him Garrett had done it, hoping he would offer to kill him, but he didn't say anything. Later, in his bedroom, he took out a porno magazine showing two people doing it doggy-style and suggested this might be more comfortable for me in my condition. It did ease the pressure on my back, but I still hoped for a little bit more. As we lay together afterward beneath his down quilt, I said, "Jennings, I'm beginning to fear for my safety."

"I can see that," he said sympathetically. We always lay sideways, facing each other and hugging. Jennings's breath smelled of peanut butter and rum.

"Don't you fear for my safety?"

He looked me straight in the eye and said, "Yes."

I touched his hair, which was curly and dark. "Jennings," I said, "are you my boyfriend?"

"Yes," he said again.

Even though he was still looking straight at me, I suspected this was a lie and began to cry. I would have cried if he'd told me the truth, too. People said all kinds of crazy things to make others believe their lives weren't as bad as they really were, and for the most part it seemed to work. Only Jonquil told the truth on a regular basis, and she was the saddest person I had ever known.

Jennings thought I was crying because of Garrett and so quickly offered to hypnotize him the following day in the boys' bathroom, using Dr. Flay's technique. I reminded him that despite my key word I was getting fatter by the minute, and suggested Jennings beat Garrett up instead—an idea he resisted. "*Larynx,*" he whispered in my ear.

"L-A-R-Y-N-X," I answered back. "*Larynx.*"

He laughed and pushed a brand-new erection up against my stomach. "No," he said. "The key word to keep Garrett from kicking you will be *larynx.*"

The next day I met Jennings in the girls' rest room before music class. He confirmed he had successfully hypnotized Garrett using a small penlight during social studies, while the rest of the class sat in the dark watching a film about nuclear war. We stood on top of a toilet seat in the mauve-colored stall, touching each other as we spoke, and Jennings made me promise to come over to his house right away after school.

In music class I turned around in my seat and said, "*Larynx!*" forcefully to Garrett, who looked back at me blankly. "Turn around, ugly," his friends said, and I did, but I took my time about it. Garrett really did look hypnotized. He looked as stupid and bland as I had imagined he might, once stripped of all his cruelty.

Mrs. Krieg put on Beethoven, and to be sure I was safe, I

turned around and whispered, *"Larynx!"* once more. Garrett wasn't even looking at me; he was noting the timpani with a pencil on his sheet music. "Shh!" Mrs. Krieg hissed at me, and I understood then that her hearing was selective.

When I went to see Jennings after school, eager to ask him how he had really made Garrett stop kicking me, Garrett himself was there, sitting on Jennings's bed. The two of them were flipping through a *Playboy* and both had erections in their pants. "Roz," Jennings said, setting the magazine aside and standing up. His penis pointed at me like the finger on an Uncle Sam poster. "I was thinking you could have sex with Garrett today instead of me. Just for today," he added hurriedly. Garrett stood up then, too, his erection pointing down at the ground. He cleared his throat and put his hands in his pockets.

"Oh," I said, trying not to sound scared. "No thanks." I stayed and talked with them for a while about nuclear holocaust, which didn't diminish their erections in the least. We all agreed germ warfare was the wave of the future, then I went home and called Jonquil. She was still at work so she couldn't talk long, but she told me not to go over to Jennings's house again, and to deny anything anyone might say about me in school from this day forward, should it come to that.

Things were okay for a while then. I ignored Jonquil's advice and continued making love with Jennings most afternoons, pretending nothing had ever happened with Garrett. In music class I stopped saying *larynx*, but Garrett didn't kick me anyway. I wondered if it had something to do with germ warfare and our shared views on that subject. I might have asked him about it had I not gone on to lose the citywide spelling bee.

"I should never have let you back into the competition!" Mrs. Googan screeched when I called to tell her the news. "Think how poor Jennings must feel right now!" I went across the street to ask him and he said he didn't give a shit. But if I wanted to make it up to him, he said, he had just gotten a new Polaroid for Christmas and needed someone to pose. I sat on his bed with my legs apart and wearing a Santa hat, like the lady from the Porta Potti. When I left I took the pictures with me, which Jennings said was no fair until I reminded him of how he had tried to sell me to Garrett. "You broke the bond of trust," I informed him, copying something Jonquil had said, and he nodded pitifully.

What neither Mrs. Googan nor I had anticipated was that my losing the semifinals would reignite Garrett's anger on behalf of Jennings. He began a campaign of kicking so strenuous that I developed a cyst on my tailbone and had to stay home from school for a week. At the end of the week, when the cyst was at its most inflamed, the doctor sliced it open and drained all the pus. He proceeded to examine me inside and out, though I had no other health complaints, after which he tersely informed my mother that my hymen was missing.

My mother demanded to know where it had gone and I quickly claimed I had been born without one. She searched my room anyway, almost as if she were looking for it, and found the Polaroid pictures of me instead. "*Sputnik* my ass!" she said, flipping through them. "You haven't lost any weight at all!" I wanted to tell her Jennings loved those pictures and that contrary to what she or Dr. Flay might think, I didn't anticipate any future problems finding men. But I didn't, of course. I watched out my bedroom window as she charged across the street to Jennings's house, pictures in hand, prepared to shock and dismay his mother.

It had been light out when my mother left to see Ms. Jennings, and it was dark when she returned. She had been crying, I could tell, and she no longer had the Polaroids. "Where are my pictures?" I demanded to know, and she looked at me like I was Jonquil.

"*Your* pictures? *Your* pictures?"

I didn't have an answer to that. While she was gone I had cooked up some Old El Paso, and now we sat down together to eat it. My mother had one taco and I went ahead and had three, since she didn't seem in the mood to count. For once she watched me eat with a kind of interest, as if she were thinking, How in the world can a thirteen-year-old eat so damn much? Somebody tell me, *please.*

I smiled at her while I was chewing and she turned stern again. "Well!" she announced suddenly. "*Your* pictures have been chopped up and placed inside Leslie Jennings's purse to be disposed of at her office, where that sorry son of hers can't retrieve them and piece them back together."

"Oh," I said. I wiped red, spicy grease from my fingers, which smelled of beef and corn.

"As for you," my mother continued, "there will be no more visits across the street."

I didn't say anything. I had no intention of going back there anyway. It was a little late, but I was planning to listen to Jonquil from now on, no matter how sad it made me.

"I'm telling you," my mother continued, "if I find out you've been over there, you'll be out on the street like your sister."

There was no point in disputing that, either, since if she did put me out, my sister would take me in and I'd be happier than ever.

I returned to school to find that Garrett had been expelled for attacking me, and that Mrs. Krieg had been replaced by Mr. Sconzo, who was fat like me and said if anyone bothered me to let him know so he could kick some booty. He listened to old American folk music instead of classical, and told us to try to enjoy the songs as a whole instead of picking out all the little bitty parts.

Jennings and I were civil in school. He asked if I would mind leaving my bedroom curtains open at night when I undressed, which I saw no harm in doing. I missed him terribly.

Three years later, as sophomores in high school, Garrett and I were in class together again. It was math, and he had changed considerably since the seventh grade, wearing round glasses and a short haircut reminiscent of John Lennon before he was killed. Beyond that, everything else about him seemed thicker and more controlled, as if he were now less inclined to commit violence, though if he got it into his head to do so, it would probably hurt a lot more.

I, too, was different. Having replaced my malfunctioning key word with an unsensible diet, compulsive exercise, and moderate vomiting, the pounds had finally begun to drop off. My mother was elated and to celebrate taught me how to shave my legs and apply makeup. The word around school was that I was now officially pretty and could finally be treated as such. I thought this would mean dates and parties, but really it just meant no one threw me into lockers anymore or called me names, which would be unseemly at our ages anyway. Ultimately the past haunted us all, and no one was prepared to nominate me for elective office or drop my name in the hat for homecoming queen. I became the leader of a group of smart quiet girls and closeted gay boys, all of us sexually frustrated.

When Garrett walked into class that day, however, I experienced an overwhelming sense of anticipation, as if his purpose in being there extended well beyond the realm of geometry. He took the empty seat behind me seemingly out of habit, and, evolved as he appeared, I could not help but find myself preparing to be assaulted. When the bell rang and this had not happened I ran to the rest room, weepy over his generous restraint and how, to my great shame, this made me love him.

Meanwhile, unbeknownst to either of us, Jennings and I had gotten puppies within a month of each other and were now meeting regularly in the street while our dogs relieved themselves on the neighbors' lawns. He complimented me on my new figure and I squeezed the biceps he was cultivating for crew. His grades had improved drastically since we had stopped making love, and his mother had seen fit to enroll him in a private high school across town. He said the girls there were nothing like me, and now that I had gotten thin he could see he was really missing out.

I told Jennings that Garrett was in my math class and he said he knew since the two of them had kept in touch after Garrett's expulsion. Apparently he had gone on to spend time in a juvenile home, where a therapist suggested it was his mother he hated and not me, and that my weight had simply provoked him into attacking me because his mother was fat, too.

"Is that true?" I asked Jennings as we walked down the street together one fall morning. The dewy air reminded me of lying in the tub with him after sex, when the mirrors were all fogged up and the whole place smelled like a greenhouse. It wasn't something I would do again, but the memory of it made me think I had made the right choice at the time.

"Absolutely," Jennings said, pulling the choke chain on his mutt, Robbie, while Edna, my miniature terrier, looked on in horror. "He feels just terrible about the mix-up."

"So that's it? He's cured?" I said.

Jennings nodded. "Probably even more so now that you've lost all this weight."

Edna sidled up to a Cutlass Supreme, sniffed the back

tire, then peed beside it. When she was finished, Robbie peed on top of her pee. Jennings and I watched without saying a word. Bodily fluids were of little consequence to the likes of us. "Well, he's good in math," I said finally, offering what little evidence I had of Garrett's reform.

Jennings turned to me then and dangled the end of Robbie's leash in my face. "You are getting very sleepy," he warned.

"What?" I said.

"Your eyelids are getting very heavy," he continued. "Soon you will fall asleep."

"Stop it, Jennings," I said, walking ahead.

He gave up and fell in step beside me. "Sorry, Roz. It's just that Garrett asked me if I would hypnotize you so you'd have sex with him in the girls' rest room."

"I see," I said, panicking slightly at the thought of being sold again.

"He says he won't hurt you if you say no, but if you just give him a chance he thinks he could make you feel really good." He put a hand in his pocket then to hide the erection he had gotten.

"I don't do that anymore," I said weakly.

"Why not?" Jennings asked, surprised. "I do."

I shifted my gaze from his crotch to his face. "With who?"

He shrugged. "Different girls."

"Well," I said, feeling suddenly morose, "hypnotism doesn't work anyway."

"Sure it does," he said. "Just look at you."

I looked at Edna instead, who was digging a small hole in Jennings's front yard, where we had ended up, while Robbie sniffed her butt. From her kitchen window, I could see Ms. Jennings peering out at us; I didn't have to look at my own house to know my mother was at her post as well. "Spell *hypnotism*," I said to Jennings for old times' sake, and he did so incorrectly, replacing the N with an M. We began to laugh, and in an instant his mother was at the front door, calling her son inside.

The next day in math class I felt a tug at the back of my hair. It was painless and affectionate and I dared not turn around.

"Yes?" Mr. Alvarez said a few minutes later, looking over my head at Garrett, who presumably had his hand up.

Garrett cleared his throat. "May I please go to the rest room?"

Mr. Alvarez nodded and Garrett got out of his seat to collect the wooden hall pass on the teacher's desk.

I waited as long as I could before asking permission to use the rest room as well.

"No," Mr. Alvarez said. "Wait until Garrett comes back."

"But I can't wait," I said. "I have to go *now*."

This was a new liberty we girls had begun to take in high school, meaning we would not be responsible for bleeding all over the classroom floor should our teachers not take heed. I had gotten my first period a month after Jennings and I stopped making love, and though I didn't have it that very day, Mr. Alvarez nodded knowingly and filled out a paper pass.

In the rest room I waited for another girl to wash her hands and leave before checking all the stalls. Garrett was in the last one, standing on the toilet seat. "*Alcatraz,*" he said softly. His voice was deeper than it had once been, his erection more forthright. He would not swim around inside me like a fish.

I stepped inside the stall and locked the door behind me. I had always been too afraid to scrutinize him before—even that time at Jennings's when we exchanged ideas about the end of the world—and so now I couldn't help but take him in. It seemed a kind of miracle that we should be so close without harm passing between us.

"*Alcatraz,*" he mentioned again after a short while, to remind me of why I was there, but he needn't have. It would be years before I would stop feeling grateful for my safety, before I would notice the ache in my tailbone warning me of unworthy men or bad weather.

For now, my only concern were the bulging blue-green veins running along his muscular forearms. As I held my breath and reached out to touch one of them, it quivered, like Edna's twiggy back legs when she was cold. I gripped the arm and used it to steady myself as I stepped up onto the toilet, where I found his cheek to be prickly and the bottoms of his earlobes like feathers between my fingertips. The hair was still yellow, and when I put my face into it and inhaled, the answer was gardenia. I held both forearms now, though I could not remember when I had taken the second one, and they gripped me protectively in return. The lips were wet and frightened as they came toward me, while inside the mouth, the teeth made tentative, idle threats.

Bikini

in 1960 i was one of the few people i knew who owned a bikini. They had been around for a while but were still considered fairly risqué. Mine was pink, made of cotton, and tied around the neck. The bottoms were nothing like the ones you see today, cut so high they seem to be missing their backs. Mine were like a pair of briefs, which was daring enough for 1960—just about the limit.

The bikini was the perfect invention for me, as I liked being naked and tried to go without clothing as often as possible. In my apartment it was easy: I could take off my clothes whenever I felt like it. In public, of course, it was harder. Sometimes the best I could do was to not wear socks. It wasn't as if

I was trying to show anything off (I didn't really have anything to show). It was more to do with feeling of a piece: waistbands seemed to cut me in half; I couldn't feel my hands beyond my cuffs.

"Put some clothes on, Vanessa," my older sister, Allison, would say when we were growing up. We shared a room, so Allison saw me naked a lot. If you'd asked me the color of her eyes back then, I couldn't have told you, for all the time she spent averting them. Allison was a prude. She always wore pajamas to bed, wouldn't talk about sex, and turned her back when she got dressed in the morning so I wouldn't see her breasts. It was the way most of the girls in the locker room at school acted, and it made me feel like we weren't sisters.

I tormented Allison with my nudity. Even in winter, when the upstairs was the coldest part of our house, I'd lie naked on top of my sheets, waiting for her to finish brushing her teeth. She'd always give a small start when she saw me, then quickly turn out the light. "I'm still naked, you know," I'd say after a few minutes in the dark.

Then Allison got pregnant while she was still in high school. My parents sent her to live with an aunt in New Jersey, and I had the bedroom all to myself. I thought about Allison a lot after that. To me, she was still a prude. If she hadn't been so uncomfortable with her body, she would've gotten herself some rubbers at the drugstore or something. I knew what happened to her would never happen to me, and it never did.

Allison didn't come home. She gave the baby up for adoption and got a job as a secretary in Manhattan. Meanwhile, I finished high school and got a scholarship to an all-girls college in upstate New York. The idea of my going to an all-girls school seemed to alarm Allison. She wrote me several letters explaining the difficulties of meeting men "on the outside," as she put it, and urging me to attend a coed college and meet "the cute and cuddly ones" while I still could. It meant a lot to me that she bothered to stay in touch, so I gave her letters some thought. In the end, I came home and enrolled in Syracuse University's School of Journalism.

Shawki and I started dating the spring of my junior year. He was an exchange student from Alexandria, brilliant not only in his field, economics, but in everyone else's, as well. He knew American politics better than we Americans did, and when any of us needed to check our facts on the Middle East we skipped the library altogether in favor of lunch with Shawki. He convinced us all that the Israelis should get out of Palestine, that the fundamentalists didn't care about Egypt's antiquities, and that the only proper way to drink tea was in a glass with lemon. Everyone wanted Shawki to come to their parties. Though his English was only so-so, he wasn't shy about mingling, and his intensity never prevented him from having a good time. He'd argue heatedly while wearing pointed party hats on either side of his head. He eagerly shared the recipe for his secret fava-bean dip.

In private Shawki was sweet, removing his glasses and turning away when I took off my clothes—not because he disapproved, as Allison had, but because he didn't know what else to do. "You are the first woman of me," he confessed shyly, and I smiled to fill the empty space he left for my confession, made years earlier to a boy named Joel in high school.

After we had been dating awhile, I wrote to Allison saying, "He's not cute and cuddly but will brilliant and sophisticated do?" I thought she would write back with something like, "That's even better," or, "Could you find one for me?" But I didn't hear from her at all until a couple of months later, when she called me out of the blue. "Is he there?" she whispered as soon as I picked up the phone.

"Allison?"

"Is he there?" she whispered again.

"Who?" I asked.

"I can't pronounce his name. Your friend."

"Shawki?"

"Yes. Is he there?"

I glanced around my apartment. I knew Shawki wasn't there, but the way Allison was whispering made me feel as if I were missing something. "No," I said.

"Good." She was speaking in her normal voice now. "I need to talk to you in private. I think you're making a mistake."

"What did I do?"

"I think you should date someone American."

"Why?"

"Why?" Allison laughed. "Don't act like you don't know, Vanessa. Don't act like you live in some separate world from the rest of us. You'll ruin your reputation, for godssakes. You'll never get married."

I looked around my apartment again. My print of van

Gogh's *Starry Night* was hanging somewhat askew, and I reminded myself to fix it later. I said, "I guess I should expect that from someone who doesn't even have a college degree."

There was silence at the other end of the line. I stared at *The Starry Night* and tried to straighten it with my mental powers, cocking my head in the direction I wanted it to go.

"He's not black, is he?" Allison asked finally. "Is he a black man?"

"No," I said, "he's light brown."

"Well, at least there's that."

I started to cry a little. Tears dripped into the holes of the telephone receiver, and for a second I wondered if I could get electrocuted. "Don't call me anymore," I said.

That night when Shawki and I made love, he asked if he had been my first. "Yes," I whispered in his ear, "of course." As soon as I said it, I was sorry. I had meant to give him something out of love, but instead it came out sounding like charity: *Of course I'd give my womanhood to you, a black man.* From that moment on, I couldn't stop feeling I had something to prove.

By summer, things had changed. Shawki had taken to going through my closet and dividing the clothes into two sections: those he liked and those he didn't like. These soon became the clothes I should wear with him and the clothes I should wear by myself; then, simply, the clothes I should and shouldn't wear. His least favorite item was a summer top with straps that tied over each shoulder. "Someone can pull the string and you will be exposed immediately," he explained, moving it to the Shouldn't side. I nodded gravely from my bed.

Still, I didn't break up with him. His distaste for exposed skin reminded me of Allison, which was vaguely comforting. I wore the shirt with the shoulder ties more and more, always leaving one of the strings loose so that it would eventually come undone. I mixed up the Shoulds and Shouldn'ts so that each time Shawki came over he had to reorder my closet. I spilled food on the Shoulds and shrank them in the dryer. I missed my sister.

That summer, Shawki built a small sailboat from a kit. He painted the hull gold and stenciled NEFERTITI in black letters on the prow, along with a freehand ankh. It was a one-man boat, really, but Shawki was sure we could both fit. "You are skinny," he told me. "It will be such that you are not really there."

We took the boat to Skaneateles Lake one Saturday to try it out. The public launch was just off East Lake Road, down a dirt path lined with weeds and trees. We drove down to the shore, unloaded the sailboat from the roof of Shawki's Fiat, then parked up the hill a ways, next to a station wagon with an empty boat trailer attached. Shawki got out of the car and examined the trailer. Patting it, he said, "Someday I will get one."

I wore my pink bikini under my shorts and T-shirt. Shawki had pronounced it a Shouldn't as soon as I'd bought it and had quickly stuffed it into the pocket of a pair of "too-tight" jeans. I took it out after he left and put it in my underwear drawer, where it brightened up all the whites and beiges. I wore the top as a bra when I knew Shawki and I would make love, and was gratified by the flash of anger that passed over his face before he quickly untied it and pulled it off me.

But today would be the first time I had worn the bikini in public. While Shawki was down by the shore raising the sail, I took off my shorts and T-shirt and tossed them in the back of the Fiat. I thought about taking off my sneakers, then remembered something Shawki had said about needing traction on a boat and changed my mind.

"Go back and put your clothes," he said when he saw me coming toward him.

I nodded and went back and got my sunglasses from the glove compartment. "How's that?" I asked when I returned.

He looked away.

"C'mon, Shawki," I said. "It's kind of funny."

He wouldn't look at me.

Shawki's mood changed once we got on the water. It turned out he was a pretty good sailor. He had never sailed before, but had read a book about it, which was just about all Shawki ever needed to do. We skimmed along the bright green lake, our sail cracking, the boat's fiberglass body showing no signs of springing a leak. Shawki slowed when we passed a house along the shore that he particularly admired. "How about that one?" he asked, shielding his eyes from the sun and pointing to a log cabin. "I take that one."

"It's okay," I said. I had tried hard all my life not to be

too impressed with Skaneateles. I loved the lake, but the wealthy town perched on its shore I could do without. When I was little and we had out-of-town guests, my parents had always brought them here—as if where we lived on Syracuse's north side wasn't good enough. "Welcome to paradise," Allison would mumble each time we smelled cow dung on the trip out—which was often—and we'd giggle in our corners of the back seat.

Shawki and I sailed toward the village of Skaneateles, a strip of shore bordered by shops and a lengthy pier. We had done well so far, managing to avoid the other boats on the lake. A race had approached at one point but Shawki had maneuvered us out of their path, calmly instructing himself in Arabic under his breath. He was becoming accustomed to the two-handed job of steering and controlling the position of the sail; my only job was to move out of the way when he wanted to put the sail where I was sitting.

I had just twisted my hair into a knot at the nape of my neck when three young men whizzed by us in a boat twice the size of ours, whistling and yelling, "Hey, hot stuff!" They were all shirtless and the one who yelled the loudest wore a captain's hat. Shawki tried to steer us away from them but he needn't have bothered; they were going much faster than we were and disappeared as quickly as they had come upon us. *Nefertiti* rocked a bit in their wake. Shawki stopped steering and let the sail go slack, leaving me to focus on the water sloshing over the edge of the boat and onto my sneakers.

"I wish to return," Shawki said suddenly.

"Why?" I asked.

"I'm tired," he said. "Ready about!"

"What?"

"I told you in the car—ready about!"

It was true: he had told me in the car. This was sailing jargon and it meant I was supposed to do something. I just couldn't remember what.

"Tell me in regular language," I said, "just this once."

"Ready about!" Shawki insisted. Then he said, "Hard-a-lee!" and hit me with the sail.

It didn't really hurt, but I was balanced so precariously on the side of the boat that it knocked me into the water. When I surfaced, I found my plastic sunglasses floating beside me. "Jesus," I said. The lake was deep and so stayed very cold, even in summer. I briefly wished for a maillot, thinking it might've quelled the sting of water on my belly.

Shawki was sailing away from me. He had turned the boat around—I now remembered what "ready about" and "hard-a-lee" were supposed to signal—and was heading back toward the launch. There was no point in panicking or calling out to him; he was just trying to scare me. I knew he would eventually come back, and he did.

What I didn't know was that he wouldn't stop. Instead, he coasted by and yelled at me, "Get up!"

I reached for the boat, but there was nothing to grab onto—no hooks, no indentations, nothing. My hands slipped right off the fiberglass. "How am I supposed to—" I hollered after him, but he wasn't listening, and since I was almost out of breath from treading water in my sneakers, I stopped calling.

He made a second pass. This time he slowed down a little, as if to be helpful. "Get up," he said again. I reached for the boat halfheartedly. Mostly I kept my eyes on him. By the time my hands slid off, I had been dragged a couple of feet.

On the third pass I just watched him go by. He didn't tell me to get up and I didn't try.

I grabbed my sunglasses, still floating nearby, and put them on. By now Shawki had put so much distance between us that I knew he wouldn't turn around again, so I excluded him from my plans. In an effort to conserve energy, I experimented with how slowly I could tread water and still stay afloat. I was hoping to save myself, and would need every ounce of strength I could muster. A last check on Shawki revealed him to be a billowy speck. He had wanted me covered up and now I was, in deep green water.

It made the most sense to head for one of the private docks near town, roughly an hour's swim. The breaststroke had always been my favorite so I went with that until my arms got tired, at which point I pitched my sunglasses and switched to freestyle. I wasn't a bad swimmer. I had joined the swim team in high school, attracted by the idea of getting to take off my clothes for educational purposes (Allison had joined the ski club). I'd even set a school record. Shawki knew this, which was probably why he felt okay leaving me in the middle of the lake.

I swam as long as I could without stopping. While my

face was in the water, I imagined Shawki turning around after all. He might have found my sunglasses on his way back and worried that I had drowned. When at last he stopped to help me back on, the glasses would be waiting for me on the boat, dried and folded.

Finally I looked up but Shawki was nowhere in sight. Or if he was somewhere in the distance, he was obscured by the bright sun and the film that coated my eyes from having opened them underwater.

At last I heaved myself onto one of the docks, my lungs burning. I stomped my feet, trying to get some of the squish out of my sneakers, and adjusted my bikini, which had shifted during the swim. I was irritated with Shawki but at the same time proud of my accomplishment: I had not needed his help getting back to shore. In fact, I did not need him at all; I would break up with him the next time I saw him.

I walked up the dock and into the backyard of a large beige house with black shutters. The grass looked untouched, and for a moment I wondered if I should take off my shoes. A brand-new picnic table sat about halfway up a slight incline, and close to it were a swing set, a jungle gym, and a red wagon, all draped in bright bows. Panting lightly, I made my way toward the house. As I passed the elevated, screened-in back porch, I heard a voice say, "Excuse me."

I stopped and looked up. A woman in her mid-twenties with a messy blond ponytail peered down at me from the porch, both hands supporting her back. She was standing as close to me as her stomach, which was touching the screen, would allow. I had visited Allison in New Jersey when she was seven months pregnant and I guessed this woman was about that far along.

"I'm sorry," I said. "I was just swimming. I didn't mean to trespass."

"Where did you get that?" the woman asked.

At first I didn't know what she meant. I didn't have anything. Then I said, "You mean my bikini?"

"Would you mind telling me?"

"No, I got it in Syracuse. The Addis Company."

"Were there any left?" she asked.

"Sure, a few."

She nodded.

"Sorry about trespassing," I said.

"I don't care," she said. She sighed. "Did you swim across the lake or something?"

"Sort of. Yeah."

"I swim at night," she said. "I don't want anyone to see me like this."

"My boyfriend pushed me off his boat," I blurted out.

"My husband's a doctor," she said.

We stood quietly for a moment until the woman abruptly said good-bye and headed back into her house. I waited until she was safely inside—as Shawki sometimes did for me when he dropped me off at my apartment—then cut through her circular driveway and woody front yard, out to East Lake Road.

The walk back to the launch was a couple of miles. I

stuck close to the trees on the shoulder, occasionally glimpsing a house through the trunks and branches. A few men whistled as they drove by, and one yelled, "Hey baby, want a ride?" but none bothered to pull over. I felt as comfortable with myself as ever in that moment, even glad Shawki had knocked me into the water. At last I was free to go, to leave him for who he was, not where he came from.

As I walked, I started thinking about my sister and the time I visited her in New Jersey. We had picked peaches from our aunt's tree and made a pie with a crisscross top. Allison ate half of it in one sitting, then burped and lifted her shirt to show me her maternity pants. She laughed and said she would keep them after the baby was born; they might come in handy over the holidays.

I had almost cried to see my sister's stomach through the stretchy white fabric that day. Now I thought I might call her tonight after breaking up with Shawki. Maybe we could work something out, I thought. Maybe I wouldn't date another exchange student.

Suddenly I had to pee, urgently. I remembered feeling the same way after swim meets at school, as if by osmosis my bladder had filled up in the pool. I ducked into the brush between houses, pulled my bottoms down, and squatted. The delicate sound of my pee hitting the dirt was periodically interrupted by the whoosh of cars just a few feet away. When I finished, I drip-dried, pulled my bottoms up, and looked briefly at the dark spot I had left on the ground. Then I headed back out to the road, where, in an instant, Shawki's boat passed me by.

At first I thought it was Shawki himself, taking this whole thing too far and leaving me in Skaneateles. But it wasn't his car; it was the station wagon we'd parked next to at the launch. Besides carrying Shawki's boat on its roof, it was pulling another boat on the trailer. But it had definitely been Shawki's boat on top. There was no mistaking that gold hull.

I ran the rest of the way back to the launch. I got more honks and whistles running, but I didn't care. I needed to get back to Shawki, to make sure he was okay—and then break it off with him.

When I found him, he was sitting on the ground near the car with his knees pulled in close to his body and his head between them. There were red marks on the sides of his calves. "What happened?" I asked, out of breath.

He looked up and I realized he wasn't wearing his glasses. It took me a couple of seconds to notice the other red mark across his cheek. "The boys take my boat," he said. His eyes were watery.

"What boys?"

"Who like your swimming suit."

I looked down at my bikini, then reached around the back and tugged at the bottoms where they had hiked up. "Let's call the police, Shawki," I said. "C'mon. Let's get to a phone."

"No," he said firmly.

"Let's get your boat back, Shawki."

"I don't want it!" he said. He stood up and looked out at the lake. "Please drive. I cannot see."

I drove us to the police station, but Shawki wouldn't go

inside. When I tried to go in alone, he grabbed my arm so tight it hurt. For as long as I'd known him, it was the only time he had ever really scared me. I started the car back up and drove us home.

Shawki was upset about the boat, but he seemed more upset that the boys who had stolen it had called him a nigger. "I tell them I am Egyptian!" he cried. "I tell them, 'Do you see this rope that you are tying my boat to your car? This rope is from me! I invent you this rope for to steal!' " They had hit him with the rope. The boy with the captain's hat had taken his glasses and thrown them in the lake. *The Captain*, Shawki called him simply: "The Captain roll down his window when he leave and tell me he will find you, Vanessa. He will find you and take you home safe."

i didn't break up with Shawki that night, nor did i call Allison. A couple of weeks later Shawki and I were still together; two years later, we were married. Nothing much ever changed between us. Shawki bought me turtlenecks for my birthday. When I got pregnant and started to show, he refused to walk down the street with me.

I did call Allison after Shawki and I divorced in 1971. She said she was sorry for the way she had acted that time long ago—that she had been bitter over her pregnancy and having been sent away and was looking for someone to punish. Her husband now, Vance, was a good man. He had two grown children from a previous marriage and made a nice living selling heated driveways. He and Allison didn't have any children of their own and enjoyed traveling in Europe.

I went to visit her in New York, where we spent hours walking around the city. My sister knew every street, timed everything so we would end up in front of the perfect bistro at lunch, the most charming tearoom in late afternoon. This was the real catching up for me: learning what Allison had learned in all that time we were apart, watching her chart her course.

Recently, while going through some old boxes, I came across my pink bikini and put it on. My daughter, Ellen, who was home from graduate school, walked in on me. I offered her the bikini and she laughed, saying even if it were in style— which it wasn't—she wouldn't be caught dead in anything that objectified women. This made me feel foolish so I took it off. "Mom!" Ellen screamed, storming out of the room. She had grown up to be more like Allison than me, and generally preferred for neither of us to see the other without clothes.

I lay down on my bed then, naked, as I had done when I was a teenager. It was hard to remember what had once made this ritual so satisfying to me, so important as to disturb my sister with it. According to Ellen, whose field was sociology, I had been a precursor to the hippies, a foreshadowing of the civil rights movements and bra burnings to come. And though politically I remained fairly savvy, she felt I had ultimately not transitioned well into the nineties, a time when people appreciated their privacy and preferred not to share as much.

"A provocative analysis," I told her, though it saddened me to recall my love affair with my body as merely a sign of the times. Rather, it had once seemed like an entire belief system to me, a political party even. At the very least it had brought me Ellen, the brown-skinned girl people were forever assuming I had adopted.

I got up and put my clothes on then. Lots of clothes. Sweaters, long johns—everything I could think of. Piled it all on. Not just because it was winter but because I could do this now; it didn't bother me. When at last I was sufficiently encumbered I scooped the bikini up off the floor, folded it as best I could, and headed for Ellen's room. She would take it, I planned to tell her. She would wear it at least once.

Almonds and Cherries

Brigitte was a nontraditional student — a polite way of saying she was thirty and not twenty-one, like the rest of the kids in her Florida film program. She was also single, childless, and possibly a lesbian, though she wasn't completely sure yet. She had unique feelings for her Intermediate Film Production professor, Shirley Mayer, who was openly gay and struck Brigitte as a sort of absentminded type who needed looking after. Mostly Brigitte thought things like it would be nice to do Shirley Mayer's laundry, or help her with her taxes. Occasionally she imagined kissing Shirley Mayer, but only occasionally, for it was a little overwhelming to feel so pleased by something so unfamiliar.

It was Brigitte's idea to explore her burgeoning sexuality on film that autumn. A recent bra-shopping trip had inspired her to write a sensual short script about a customer and the sales associate helping her, all of which would take place in a dressing room. (A minimal number of locations, Shirley Mayer had instructed the class, would be cheaper and less strenuous in terms of moving equipment.) Brigitte turned in the requisite treatment for 36C only to get it back from Shirley Mayer unmarked and with a note at the top saying to please see her.

"What is this?" Shirley Mayer asked Brigitte during office hours that afternoon. She was sitting at her desk holding Brigitte's treatment, which she had quickly reread before posing the question. Shirley Mayer was a pink-faced blonde in a stylish gray suit with black buttons who never, ever removed her jacket.

"It's my script," Brigitte said. She shifted in her seat and recrossed her legs, feeling suddenly underdressed in jeans.

"Jesus," Shirley Mayer said. "You too."

"Me too?"

Shirley Mayer handed Brigitte back her treatment. "The whole class is writing about being gay," she said. "We'll screen these films for the parents at the end of the year, and I'll get fired for converting you all."

"I'm not converted," Brigitte said, immediately wishing she could take it back.

"Well, that's a relief," Shirley Mayer snapped.

"What if the films were all good?" Brigitte asked quickly. "I mean, festival quality?"

Shirley Mayer shook her head. "They're not," she said. "Yours is the best one."

Brigitte smiled. "Thank you."

"It's flattering, you know? All this gay pride. But it's going to get me fired."

"I could make a different film," Brigitte offered.

Shirley Mayer waved this away. "No, no," she said, laughing. "Make your film. I really only called you in here to tell you I liked your treatment."

"You probably won't get fired," Brigitte said.

"Probably not," Shirley Mayer said.

"I'm a nontraditional student," Brigitte blurted out.

"Yes," Shirley Mayer said, smiling. "That's admirable."

On the drive home, Brigitte thought about how she didn't want Shirley Mayer to get fired, but how if it did happen, it would be Shirley Mayer's own fault. She was pretty and charismatic and had seduced them all with her practical knowledge, thought-provoking exercises, and unfriendly demeanor.

On the first day of class, for example, she had offered a third of them chocolates from a huge See's Candies assortment. She offered a second third of them chocolates as well, but this time from a somewhat less varied assortment containing only dark fruit creams. The students in the last third were offered a choice between marshmallow creams and toffees. Afterward, when Shirley Mayer asked them what they thought the exercise meant, they responded—mouths full—that they didn't know. "You," she said then, pointing to Ely Gimble, who had been in the first third. "You took forever to decide."

Ely nodded. "Are there any fruit creams left?" he asked, and Shirley Mayer absently handed him the box.

"And you," she said, pointing to Brigitte, who had been in the last third. "What was your experience?"

"I chose faster," Brigitte said immediately, desperate even then to make an impression.

"That's right," Shirley Mayer said, nodding. "And so my point is?" she asked, looking first to Brigitte, then to the rest of the class. Nobody said anything. "What about you?" she asked Paige Cox, who had been in the middle group. "State your name and describe your experience, please."

"Paige. I don't like chocolate."

"But you picked one," Shirley Mayer said.

"I'm going to give it to someone else," Paige said. Then she added, "To my girlfriend."

Two boys in the back of the room giggled.

"What's funny, guys?" Shirley Mayer asked them.

They sat up straight in their chairs and turned instantly, mockingly solemn. "Um," Davis Bonaire said, "that she's a lesbian?"

Everyone looked at Shirley Mayer, who they already knew to be gay. She paused briefly before saying, "Take out a sheet of paper, please."

"Who, me?" Davis asked.

"Yes, you," Shirley said. "And your friend. What's your name?"

"Jojo," Jojo Mankowski said.

"And you, Jojo. Take out a sheet of paper."

The two boys shuffled their notebooks and came up with some paper. When they were ready, Shirley Mayer said, "Now, please write a hateful letter to Paige."

"Excuse me?" Davis said.

"This isn't high school, you know," Jojo said. "We're paying for this class. If we want to be taught a lesson, we'll call our mothers."

"Lesson?" Shirley Mayer said. "What lesson? I would like you both to write a hateful letter to Paige, please, so I can get on with this lecture."

Paige turned around then and looked at the two of them. "Yeah," she said. "Write me a hateful letter."

Davis and Jojo looked at each other. "I ain't doing that," Davis said, laying his pen on the desk.

"Me neither," Jojo said, copying Davis.

Shirley Mayer shrugged. "Suit yourselves," she said. "Just trying to be accommodating."

Paige turned back around then and smiled at Shirley Mayer, who ignored her. "Now," Shirley Mayer said, "getting back to the chocolate. What was the purpose?"

Jojo Mankowski raised his hand. "Yes?" Shirley Mayer said, pointing to him.

"It's easier to choose when you've got less to choose from," he said.

"Good man!" Shirley Mayer said. "I want you all to remember that now as I pass out my list of creative limitations. They're designed to help you, not make your lives harder."

The list was called the "Mayer Memorandum" and consisted of six guidelines, all beginning with the letter *M*: no machine guns, no monkeys, no mission impossibles, no Mafia, no murder, no madness.

"You got something against action movies?" a guy named Benny Parisi asked her.

"Yes," Shirley Mayer said. "Any other questions?"

Brigitte raised her hand then. "Is the monkey literal or figurative?"

"Let's not overanalyze," Shirley Mayer told her. When no one else raised their hand she asked, "Everyone unhappy now?" They all nodded except Brigitte and Paige. "Good!" Shirley Mayer said. "Then things can only get better."

"Damn!" Davis Bonaire said and, quite unexpectedly, he began to laugh, followed by the rest of the class, and finally Shirley Mayer.

Brigitte's movie was about a young woman who goes bra shopping and finds she likes the way the sales associate touches her skin. The sales associate fastens the young woman's bras even though the young woman has been fastening her own bras all her life, then smooths her hand across the young woman's shoulder. At the sales associate's suggestion, the young woman tries on more bras than she'd intended—some violet, some lacy, some push-up—but only buys a couple of plain white ones in the end. As she pays for them, a young man approaches the sales associate and kisses her. The young woman looks questioningly at the sales associate, who looks away. "Come back and see us," the sales associate says meaningfully when she hands the young woman her receipt.

This had happened to Brigitte in real life, and when she'd described the event to Raoul, her stocky French roommate, he had suggested she write it all down and submit it to *Penthouse Forum*. "Just forget about the guy at the end and make the women get it on in the dressing room," he'd added.

Now, on a warm Saturday in September, Brigitte and Raoul sat together at their pink Formica kitchen table, watching the smoke from Raoul's cigarette mix with the morning sunlight. Raoul wore boxer shorts and extremely short, dyed blond hair, while Brigitte was in dirty Levi's, with no bra underneath her T-shirt. "I wonder sometimes," Raoul said, watching the swirly, smoking air, "if this type of effect would register on film."

"You probably wouldn't want it to," Brigitte said. "It's kind of prosaic."

"Prosaic?" Raoul said.

"*Prosaïque*," Brigitte said, translating.

Raoul, understanding now, was dismissive. "You Americans," he said. "Always trying to invent something new. The trick is to learn to live with the banal."

"You French," Brigitte said. "Always bugging the shit out of me."

Raoul laughed and kissed Brigitte on both cheeks before heading for the garden shed in the backyard, where he lifted weights every morning. He had graduated from the film program the year before and now spent most of his time body-building and bartending. Occasionally a local band would ask him to shoot a music video for them and Raoul would do it in return for beer or pot. Sometimes he did it for free. Film school, he liked to say, had taught him more about how to watch films than how to make them, and so this was his main focus at the moment.

Brigitte and Raoul had moved in together as lovers, but when that didn't work out, they were loath to separate since they were such compatible roommates. So she took the second bedroom in the small house they rented, while Raoul relocated his weight-lifting apparatus to the tin shed from Sears. They were only slightly jealous of one another when a third party entered the equation, and occasionally fell into bed together under extenuating circumstances, like when Brigitte told Raoul about her bra-shopping trip. "Shit, man," he had complained to her. He called everybody *man*. "You got me horny."

Afterward, in bed, Brigitte asked him if he would shoot 36C for her. "Two girls getting it on?" he said, lighting a cigarette. "No problem." It had taken Brigitte a long time to figure out that even though everything that came out of Raoul's mouth was sexist, he himself was not. This was confusing, though, and his attitude had lost him several female friends over the years. "You don't understand, man," he would say in his own defense. "I love women!" Something must have gotten lost in the translation was all Brigitte could think. As she understood it, Raoul's suggestion that she publish in *Penthouse Forum* was really a testament to her storytelling abilities; his agreeing to film two girls getting it on meant lesbians were okay with him.

Still, Raoul had a hard time believing that Brigitte herself might be gay. "Everybody loves Shirley Mayer," he once told her. "Don't take it so personally. Besides, you fuck like a maniac!"

"Maybe I'm bi," Brigitte said.

"Everybody's bi."

"You're bi?"

He shrugged then. "Maybe. If I thought about it. I just don't think about it. I prefer women, man. It's easier that way."

Which pretty much summed up the problem with Raoul for Brigitte. He did whatever was easiest, no matter how much harder it might make things for him in the future. Not that he really was gay, or even bisexual. He wasn't. But he was a halfway decent cinematographer who wasted his time serving beer for a living; a fitness freak who could not see the harm in a little pot.

For Brigitte it was better to know the truth up front. If she was gay, so be it. If she wasn't, she would sort her way through that mess, too. But she hoped she was. She hoped beyond hope that her problems were at last about to become interesting.

Brigitte received an inordinate amount of help on her film from Jojo Mankowski. He worked part-time in a department store and lobbied one of his managers to let Brigitte shoot 36C in the lingerie department. "Just so you know, I told him it was about shoplifting," Jojo informed her before the shoot. "I didn't think he'd go in for all that homo shit."

Brigitte nodded. Now that she knew the entire class was making gay-themed films she felt safer with them—even people like Jojo and Davis Bonaire, who himself had offered to record sound for her, one of the least popular jobs on a film set. The two of them still had a tendency to sound foul when they spoke on sensitive topics, but Brigitte decided they probably suffered from an affliction similar to Raoul's—one in which their mouths did not accurately represent their beliefs.

They shot on two consecutive Sunday mornings, before the department store opened at noon. Paige Cox played the role of the young woman buying the bras, while her girlfriend, Andie Rivette, played the sales associate. Benny Parisi played the boyfriend who comes in and kisses the sales associate at the end, but would only agree to do so after Brigitte assured him Andie wasn't butch. "It's gotta look like I'm really kissing a girl," he warned. "My parents are gonna see this." And everyone enjoyed working with Raoul who, though no longer in the program, remained famous for a film about a nude woman who enlists a detective agency to help her find her clothes. It was shot almost entirely from the actors' necks up, so there was no on-screen nudity—just heads bobbing along the bottom of the frame and crazy scenery filling the space above them.

In the end Raoul proclaimed Brigitte's shoot a success because Paige and Andie had been *hot* together. "They're the real thing, man," he said, grabbing his crotch. "You can feel it right here!" He and Brigitte had loaded the last of the school's camera equipment into the bed of his truck and were headed home now, exhausted. Mercifully the temperature had dropped out of the nineties and they were enjoying the breeze, as opposed to Raoul's air conditioner.

"Yeah, but some of that's directing," Brigitte protested, dangling an arm outside her open window.

"But of course it is! You did a great job, man. I'm just complimenting you on the casting, too."

Brigitte was dissatisfied. "What I'm saying is," she said, turning to face him as he drove, "how could I possibly have made a good lesbian film if I wasn't a lesbian?"

Raoul laughed and kept his eyes on the road. "Oh honey," he said, which he only called her when he was about to deliver bad news, "because you're talented."

Shirley Mayer gave Brigitte an A+ on the film. In her comments she called it sexy, funny, sad, and true to life. Her favorite part was a close shot of the sales associate's index finger passing over a raised mole on the young woman's back. "Great texture," Shirley Mayer wrote. At the bottom of the paper she added, "Please see me."

Brigitte arrived at Shirley Mayer's office thinking Shirley Mayer was going to pronounce her a lesbian, or at least ask her if she was one, then maybe try to help her come out. Instead she seemed irritated, as if she hadn't remembered it was she who had asked Brigitte to come in the first place. For a few moments neither of them spoke beyond initial pleasantries, which reminded Brigitte of therapy and how she could never think of an appropriate opening remark. Often she just burst out crying, or else said something garish like, "I've been tightening up during intercourse." Today with Shirley Mayer, she suddenly found herself saying, "If you saw my film and didn't know me, would you think I was gay?"

Shirley Mayer pounced on this. "What's the matter? You afraid of being pigeonholed?"

"Of course not," Brigitte began, but Shirley Mayer cut her off.

"You live with that French guy, don't you? Just make sure you say that in all your interviews, right up front: 'I live with a man!' You should be fine then."

"But I wouldn't mind being pigeonholed," Brigitte said.

Shirley Mayer picked up a paper clip from her desk blotter and threw it at a bookcase across the room. "Oh hell," she said. "I know you wouldn't."

Brigitte paused for a moment before asking, "Is something wrong?"

Shirley Mayer sighed. "It was a plot. All those gay scripts. Jojo Mankowski devised a plot whereby everyone would write a gay script and say I made them do it."

"No, he didn't," Brigitte said, only because she considered herself to be somewhat inside the loop and had heard no such thing.

"In fact he did," Shirley Mayer said.

Brigitte didn't say anything.

"I have to assume that neither you nor Paige were in on it."

"Of course not," Brigitte said.

"Then why did you write that movie? About the bras? That's what I'd like to know."

"It's based on a true story," Brigitte said.

"Yes," Shirley Mayer said. "Most things are. I'm asking, why did you pick that particular story? You want me to know it's okay with you that I'm gay?"

"No," Brigitte said. She shifted in her seat.

"Trying to make me feel at home in a room full of right-wing southerners?"

"No!"

"Oh hell," Shirley Mayer said again, and she threw another paper clip across the room. "I know why you wrote it."

Why? Brigitte wanted to ask, but instead she said, "Are you going to get fired?"

"God no!" Shirley Mayer said. "I have proof. A falsified 'Mayer Memorandum' that begins with 'No men and women together.' No, being persecuted at a state institution is probably the best thing that could have happened to me. You can't do much better than that."

Brigitte cleared her throat. "Would you like to have dinner with me sometime?"

Shirley Mayer didn't respond immediately. She repositioned her desk blotter first, then sharpened a brand-new pencil. At last she did something Brigitte had never seen her do, which was to unbutton her suit coat. It fell open to reveal that she wore no bra beneath her off-white silky blouse, and that her breasts were small and round, with pale nipples. "Your movie fascinated me, Brigitte," she said. "I burned my bras in 1972 and never bought new ones. Now I just wear these stupid coats. It's all the same, though, isn't it?"

Brigitte didn't know what to say.

"Making ourselves presentable," Shirley Mayer added.

Brigitte nodded then. "Yes. I see."

"But now women like wearing bras, right?"

"I guess if you have a large chest it might be more comfortable," Brigitte said, trying not to be obvious about appreciating Shirley Mayer's breasts.

"Oh really?" Shirley Mayer asked. "Is that how you find it?"

Brigitte resituated herself in her chair. "Well, yes."

Shirley Mayer nodded. "My point," she said finally, "is that it's a fashion."

"Oh," Brigitte said.

"A passing fancy."

"I see."

"Which brings me back to your movie."

"It does?"

Shirley Mayer began buttoning her coat back up. "Your movie deals with something I like to call the temporary lesbian."

Brigitte watched as the last of Shirley Mayer's breasts disappeared.

She continued: "The temporary—or environmental—lesbian feels attracted to other women only in specialized, often isolated situations, where she doesn't run the risk of condemnation from the general public. I mean, she's not the sort of person who finds herself getting into trouble over her sexuality. She simply isn't that committed."

"Oh," Brigitte said. "I guess that wasn't really what I had in mind."

"Nevertheless," said Shirley Mayer, "the film succeeds brilliantly at that level. In fact, I know several people who I'm sure would be very interested in seeing it."

Brigitte nodded weakly. "I'll make you a copy."

Shirley Mayer smiled. "Thank you," she said. "And thank you for the dinner invitation. Really. I accept. Just give me a rain check until the end of the semester, after I turn my grades in. Then you, the French guy, and I will all go out and have dinner."

"Shirley Mayer thinks i'm a fake," Brigitte told Raoul that night. She had gone to see him at work, a sunken bar in an old bowling alley behind a shopping center.

"How so?" Raoul asked, handing her a glass of beer. He had showered and was sharply dressed in a mod-looking black T-shirt, which usually meant he hoped to go home with one of his patrons after work. Brigitte could tell she was cramping his style from the way he kept glancing down the bar at two giggling brunettes, but she didn't care. She had no one else to talk to.

"She thinks I'm in a phase."

"A gay phase?" Raoul asked.

"I think so."

He shrugged. "Maybe you should listen to her."

"Why?" Brigitte asked, indignant.

"Because man, she's probably right."

Brigitte sighed. "But I'm proposing that my heterosexuality is the phase."

"This is too long to be a phase! The phase must be the shorter period of the two. You've only been gay for three months, so this must be the phase."

The two brunettes got up and left. "Shit, man," Raoul grumbled.

"Sorry," Brigitte said.

He leaned on the bar then and lowered his eyelids in a way he knew she found sexy. "Want to make it up to me?"

"No."

"Shit, man," he said again, opening his eyes back up and straightening out his spine. "Why don't you go bowl or something? You're too good-looking. You scare away my piece of ass!"

He left to make drinks for a middle-aged couple who had taken the brunettes' stools and were still outfitted in bowling shoes. Brigitte finished her beer and rented a pair of shoes herself. She got a lane and bowled three games alone, each time increasing her score by roughly twenty points. She had just started bowling a fourth when one of the brunettes approached her, an amber beer bottle in her left hand. "Hi," the woman said.

Brigitte had been standing over the ball return, trying to decide between an elegantly marbled green ball and a plain black one that was easier to carry. "Hi," she said now, thinking she had an idea of what was about to come. It had happened before—women interested in Raoul wanting to know first if Brigitte was his girlfriend and, if not, would she mind introducing them?

Instead the brunette asked, "How're the bras?"

"The bras?" Brigitte said.

"I sold you some bras a few months ago. At Dillard's."

Brigitte stopped and took a closer look at the woman. She would have to take her word for it, she decided, for it suddenly occurred to Brigitte that she had spent most of that afternoon in the dressing room with her eyes closed. As much as she had enjoyed their sensual experience, the sight of the two of them in the mirror had made her somewhat uncomfortable. "Oh right," she said after a moment. "Right."

"Is it Brigitte?" the woman asked.

"Yes," Brigitte said, trying desperately to conjure up a name other than Tammy, the one she had given the sales associate character in 36C.

"I'm Hazel," the brunette said, helping out.

"Sorry," Brigitte said. "I knew there was a z in it."

Hazel smiled. "Anyway, I thought that was you at the bar."

"That was me," Brigitte said. "I was talking to my roommate," she added quickly.

Hazel nodded and took a seat at the electronic scoring table facing the lanes. Meanwhile, Brigitte picked up the green bowling ball and tried to act as if it were very light. After a few seconds she put it back down again, then proceeded to dry her hands over the air blower.

"So how are those bras working out for you?" Hazel asked.

"Great," Brigitte said. "They're great."

Hazel smiled again. "I'm glad." The lane next to Brigitte's was unoccupied and so Hazel stood up and walked over to the other side of the ball return, facing Brigitte now. She took a swig of beer and covered her mouth to veil a small burp. Brigitte thought she must have been about twenty-five, and noticed that her pelvic bones protruded slightly from her snug, faded jeans.

"Maybe you'd better get off the bowling floor," Brigitte said, noticing Hazel's clogs. "They're kind of strict about shoes here."

Hazel followed Brigitte's eyes down to her feet and said, "Oops." She stepped down from the wooden platform and returned to the scoring bench.

"You could rent some shoes," Brigitte said. "I mean, I didn't mean to kick you out or anything." No matter how long she dried them, her hands seemed to keep sweating.

"It's okay," Hazel said. "I'm really just here for my friend. She likes your roommate."

Brigitte nodded.

Suddenly Hazel looked concerned. "I can tell her to lay off if you want. I mean, if the two of you are more than roommates."

"Oh no," Brigitte said. "He's just a friend."

Hazel nodded.

"He's just French," Brigitte said.

Hazel stood up again. She looked at the scoring monitor overhead, which had been indicating it was Brigitte's turn to bowl for several minutes now. "Do you think my friend has a chance with him?" she asked Brigitte.

"Oh sure," Brigitte said. She hit the reset button next to the hand dryer and the eight pins she had once hoped to convert into a spare got knocked down. She sensed her options in terms of activity on the bowling floor diminishing rapidly, and yet she felt uncertain about stepping off it.

"Maybe we could hang out while my friend talks to your roommate," Hazel suggested.

"Sure."

"I don't really want to bowl," she said.

"That's okay."

"I could watch you bowl."

"Oh."

"I was watching you before so I could just keep watching you."

"I see," Brigitte said.

Hazel laughed a little. "I was spying on you," she said.

Brigitte laughed, too. "Well," she said. "Hmm."

Hazel set her beer down on the scoring table. She said, "Your bra strap is showing," and stepped up onto the bowling floor to fix it. Though Brigitte kept her eyes open this time, she remembered Hazel better from the soft pads of her fingertips, the smell of almonds and cherries that came off her face.

They all ended up back at Brigitte and Raoul's place. Almost immediately Raoul and Mary Louise, Hazel's friend, disappeared inside the tin shed in the backyard. After hearing that this was where Raoul kept his weights, Mary Louise—whose biceps were minute but bulgy—had insisted she be given the opportunity to prove she could bench-press a hundred pounds.

That left Brigitte and Hazel in the living room, a square space with a wooden floor, a futon, and two red director's chairs. "Matching chairs," Hazel commented as she settled herself into the one bearing Brigitte's name. "How romantic."

Brigitte took a seat on the futon. "They're old," she said. "We've had them for, like, three years."

Hazel nodded.

"We paid for them ourselves. They weren't gifts to each other or anything."

"I like the color," Hazel said.

"If we ever actually used them on a student shoot people would probably laugh at us."

Hazel looked blankly at Brigitte, who was desperately trying to stop talking about the chairs. "Here," Brigitte said suddenly, hopping up from the futon. She walked over to the

TV and popped in a videocassette of *36C*. "Here's something," she said.

They watched the movie in silence. Brigitte failed to return to her seat, instead standing next to the TV for the duration of the film, ready to shut it off should Hazel experience any discomfort.

But she seemed to like it, clapping and saying "Bravo" when it was over.

"Really?" Brigitte asked her. She hit rewind on the VCR.

Hazel nodded. "I'm flattered."

Brigitte ejected the tape and carried it back to the futon with her. "Wow," she said.

"Assuming that's me, of course. I mean, us."

Brigitte nodded. "Raoul shot it."

"Raoul seems interesting," Hazel said, which Brigitte took to mean she didn't like him, a fairly common occurrence among thinking women.

"He's French," Brigitte said.

"You mentioned that."

"I was wondering," Brigitte said, "do you think I'm gay?"

Hazel laughed. "I hope so," she said.

"Are you?" Brigitte asked.

"Uh-huh."

"Who was that guy who kissed you in the department store?"

Hazel sighed. "My ex-boyfriend. He's having a hard time making the transition."

"Hmm," Brigitte said.

"I'm not," Hazel assured her.

"Oh," Brigitte said. "That's good."

Hazel smiled. She looked out the window at the tin shed, whose silver sides were reflecting moonlight. "Is Mary Louise safe with him?" she asked.

"Absolutely," Brigitte said.

"You know him from the film program?"

Brigitte nodded. "He introduced me to Shirley Mayer."

"Who's she?" Hazel asked, and Brigitte told her about how Shirley Mayer wore jackets instead of bras, how she had been persecuted and would now get to keep her job forever.

"But she shouldn't have done that," Hazel said.

"Done what?" Brigitte asked.

"Shown you her breasts."

"Why not?"

Hazel shrugged. She said, "I shouldn't have touched your shoulders that day in the department store, either."

"Oh," Brigitte said, gravely disappointed.

"Or maybe I should have," Hazel said. "I don't know."

"It seemed fine to me," Brigitte said.

"You're supposed to feel safe in a dressing room."

"I did feel safe."

"You kept closing your eyes."

"I was safe," Brigitte insisted.

"It's just that you seem sort of impressionable."

"I'm thirty, for godsakes," Brigitte told her. "I'm a non-traditional student."

Hazel nodded. "I'm sorry."

"Shirley Mayer taught me who I am."

"So you're in love with her?"

"I want to take care of her," Brigitte corrected.

"I see," Hazel said. She stood up then and stretched her arms.

Brigitte stood up, too. "Don't leave yet," she said.

Hazel laughed. She moved toward Brigitte, tugged on the waistband of her jeans, and asked for a tour of the house.

In the bedroom they kissed for a long time, first softly, politely—as if they were related—then more invasively. They were still standing after twenty minutes or so when Hazel complained of the heat and took off Brigitte's shirt. Underneath was the plain white bra she had sold Brigitte a couple of months earlier, which she quickly pushed up instead of removing, pleasing Brigitte with her urgency.

"Do you like it like this?" Hazel asked, taking off her own shirt now. "Without the dressing room?" She wore one of the violet lace bras from the department store, the kind that lifted little breasts. She took that off, too, and reached down to unbutton her jeans. "Do you like it without Shirley Mayer?" she whispered.

"Yes," Brigitte said. She moved closer to Hazel now—much, much closer—and suddenly found herself possessed of a profound appreciation for moisture and fragrance, a refined sense of geography as it applied to those areas of the body women shared. And she felt, from Hazel's reactions, that she had a knack for this sort of thing. For the first time in her life the generosity aspect of sex had ceased to feel like work to her. She thought she might go on forever.

When at last Hazel insisted it was her turn to be generous,

Brigitte lay back tentatively, but then asked Hazel to stop. It wasn't because what Hazel was doing felt like nothing, she tried to explain, but rather, it was too much of something. The right thing. That which would have to be worked slowly into her system so as to trick her into thinking it had been there all along, as opposed to overwhelming her with the torrid fact of its long, unwarranted absence.

iN the m<0>rNiNg Brigitte aNd Hazel were sitting at the kitchen table, drinking coffee and occasionally reaching inside each other's shirts, when Raoul wandered in from the backyard. "Where's Mary Louise?" Hazel asked him. He wore no shoes and was opening and closing kitchen cupboards in search of something.

"In the shack, man," he said. Then he added, "Shit, Brigitte, where's my aloe vera?"

Brigitte got up from the table and helped him look. "What do you need aloe vera for?" Hazel said. "Is Mary Louise okay?"

Raoul laughed. "Mary Louise is fine. She cut me with her nails, man. You want to see my back?"

"No thanks," Hazel said.

"Here," Brigitte said, handing Raoul the tube of salve. "It was in the junk drawer."

Raoul nodded. "Thanks, man," he said. Then he kissed her on both cheeks, as he had done every morning of their life together.

Hazel looked away and, seeing this, Raoul shrugged. "Hey, man," he said to her. "I'm French."

"Man?" Hazel said.

"Okay," Raoul said, "I'm French, *'A-zel*. This is how we say 'ello, good morning, whatever."

"Kiss Hazel," Brigitte said.

"I think she doesn't want me to," Raoul protested, shoving his hands in his pockets.

"As long as Mary Louise is all right, it would be okay," Hazel said.

Raoul was momentarily still, then took his hands out of his pockets and leaned down to kiss Hazel's cheeks. As he did, his shirt pulled up a bit at the back, and Brigitte could see some of the red welts Mary Louise's nails had left on his skin. Not scratches or scrapes, but bitter little half-moons outlined in dried blood. Imprints. At first Brigitte was appalled at Mary Louise, then fleetingly jealous of her, then, oddly, gratified. She must have been as strong as she had claimed, Brigitte decided at last. Raoul should have believed her.

Lass

it was a cold march night and they sat across the bar from each other, smiling over the fact that they both kept ordering Guinness. Silently they competed, in an attempt to drink each other under a table they didn't share. "You won," he told her later, on his way back from the toilet. He said his name was Carl and apologized immediately for being so fat. She told him it wasn't that bad, and really it wasn't. He expressed surprise that an American should have such a taste for the brown stuff, and Shayna said why shouldn't she, it tasted good.

Carl described himself as being no different from any other Irishman in London, working an office job he never would have found in Dublin and wishing he could go home, particularly when the natives got restless and it was Paddy this and Paddy that on the train platforms, at the kiosks, in the queues for sausage and chips. Shayna explained that she was on a work permit through her American university, earning high pay for her excessive typing skills. When Carl asked her how it was that he had gotten so lucky as to meet her, she neglected to tell him that she frequently drank alone, and tonight was no different.

As the evening wore on, Shayna noted many fine qualities in Carl: generosity, humor, sportsmanship, the fine accent, the gray eyes. Quite simply, he meant her no malice and she appreciated the gesture. When the pub closed they shook hands as a show of restraint.

Carl had told her who his father was, and Shayna had been careful not to mention her inability to get through the man's books. She decided the blame must lie with her since she was American and it was her heritage not to be able to pay attention. The next day she bought one of Niall Meara's novels, thinking the outlay of cash might make his writing more interesting. It didn't, but she spent some time manhandling the volume and dog-earing pages, in anticipation of a visit from the son.

Carl stayed at Shayna's place on their second date, the two of them having just seen a French film. It was a tiny room in North London, big enough for a twin bed, a dresser, and a freestanding wardrobe. The landlord had provided a synthetic pink bedspread, and as Shayna and Carl lay naked beneath it, he again regretted his size. "This weight," he said. "It's like when I came over on the boat, I never set my luggage down."

Shayna sucked in her stomach to help create an illusion of space. She and Carl lay facing each other, and now he studied her, concerned. "Breathe," he commanded after a moment, and she let her stomach escape her, nestling itself lightly against his own. "Try this," he said, turning away from her to lie on his side. "See if you have more room this way."

She curled up behind him and smelled his back, which was not at all dank or sweaty. Carl saw his father's book then, lying on the floor where Shayna had so carefully positioned it, and said, "You read this shite?"

Later he turned around and asked her to do the same, so that he faced her back. She did, and now he was smelling her skin, kissing it, gently separating her thighs. Throughout the night he awakened her, pressing up against her and asking quietly if she felt ready again. He said he had never known it could be like this, the woman facing away and enjoying herself, and Shayna was pleased. She had practiced for several years, training herself to like the things men looked at in pictures, and now she liked them. She thought men had it right, keeping things vaguely anonymous the way they did.

For their third date they decided on a German film. Shayna took the tube to Hampstead, a quaint area featuring ivy and pouring rain, and waited outside the theater until Carl never showed.

She bought a ticket anyway and watched the film from the back of the auditorium, standing there until her legs cramped and people began running into her on their way out to the rest rooms. When she finally took a seat, blocking people's views and irritating them with the inescapable cellophane of her candy bar, she couldn't seem to stop turning around. "Carl?" she called, as someone opened the auditorium doors, spreading light across the aisles, and a voice from behind her bellowed, "Forget it, love! He's not coming!" Others laughed and still others told them to hush. Later, walking the night streets beneath her dripping umbrella, all Shayna could remember of the movie was a sheet of filmy paper drifting listlessly through the air, a sickly man entranced by the spectacle of it.

She took the train to north London, not bothering to put her umbrella up on the walk from the tube station to her flat. The smell of clove cigarettes enticed her to stop in at the neighborhood pub, where another Irishman bought her drinks, and used his bar napkin to dry her hair and face. Normally she could be had this easily, but not tonight, not until she squared things with Carl.

The Irishman asked to walk Shayna home and graciously accepted her decline, though he proceeded to follow her at a short distance. She liked the sound of his boot steps quickening and then slowing with hers, and imagined he thought she was oblivious. This type of thing had happened to her before, and Shayna regretted not having the sense to feel worse about it, the instinct to protect herself.

But as she turned into her gate, he slowed, then walked

on past the house. He had seen Carl before she did, waiting for her on the front steps, hands tucked inside his bomber jacket. "Shayna," he said, "I'm so sorry I was late tonight. But I was there, I swear." From his pocket he produced a torn ticket stub, candy wrappers, a scribbled summary of the film. Had Shayna stayed until the lights came up, she would have found him in an aisle seat not far from her own.

They hugged. Shayna sank into Carl's largeness and noticed that, like her, he had been drinking; like her, he was grateful for their reunion. And yet in the end, she believed he was better than she. She believed his father made him better, and that she would be made better, too, by an involvement with either one of them. Because there were things wrong with her: the way she brought home strangers, her drinking maybe, how she couldn't concentrate on books.

Carl and Shayna were married in June by the borough of Islington registrar. Carl refused to invite his father, citing an early novel disparaging of a fat son as evidence of the man's unworthiness. "What about your mother?" Shayna asked, and he dismissed her out of hand as a co-conspirator. He had an older sister, Sheila, but she was in America of all places, getting what Carl described as her touchy-feely degree, which was really a doctorate in psychology.

Shayna invited her own mother, who wanted to come but was afraid of crossing the Atlantic in a plane, and her father, who, as Paris bureau chief of an American newspaper, was relatively close by. However, he declined, feeling awkward at events requiring physical contact, such as graduations or confirmations. Still, he was compelled by his profession to congratulate her on marrying into a literary family, and offered to wire money were she to name a reasonable sum.

After the ceremony, Carl and Shayna left their jobs and used her father's money to take an extended honeymoon on the west coast of Ireland. "Meara?" the spindly proprietress of their bed-and-breakfast asked when they gave their last name. "You wouldn't be related to himself now, would you?" Carl surprised Shayna by answering that they would. It was a small village, and once word got out that Niall Meara's son was there on his honeymoon, people stopped charging them for things. Not only did they get their bed-and-breakfast from Mrs. Riordan, but lunch and dinner as well. Drinks at the pub were on the house (though the barman fretted over Carl's intake affecting his "performance"), and a nearby shearer sent over a scratchy tartan blanket with many happy returns. The local paper took a photo of the newlyweds and wrote a small piece to accompany it, and they were generally assured by all that this was the least the village could do, Niall Meara having brought them so much pleasure over the years.

In the days that followed they froze themselves walking barefoot through the surf, then climbed any number of seaside cliffs to get their circulation back, Carl hauling the blanket over his shoulder. In the tall, fragrant weeds at the top they laid it down, then wrapped themselves tightly inside. The trick, Carl whispered, curved around her back and clearing any unnecessary clothing from between them, was to look like they were just resting, like they had nothing to hide. She wore dresses to make things easier for him and, as they lay connected, listened to the hidden rustles of the children who followed them at a distance.

A phone call came as the honeymoon neared its close, and it was with great pride that, upon their return from the cliffs one evening, Mrs. Riordan announced she'd had the privilege of speaking with Niall Meara himself, all the way from Dublin. Carl thanked her for the message, then turned to go upstairs. "Are you not going to ring him back?" she called after him, standing beside the telephone table in the foyer, but he ignored her.

In the bedroom, Carl tossed the tartan blanket onto an antique chair and sat down at the edge of their wood-frame bed. He was always a little flushed from their afternoons together, but today it seemed this was more agitation than love. "What should I do?" he asked Shayna, but she couldn't say. She only knew what she hoped he would do, and that might not have been the right answer. "You ring him," Carl said finally.

"Me?" Shayna said.

"Ring him and tell him you're my wife and you're beautiful and you could have had any bloke you wanted and you picked me."

"But I can't do that," she said.

"Well," he said, and he laughed in a choked way she had never heard before. "I guess you were bound to tell me no sometime."

Shayna was instantly stricken, and reached out a hand to steady herself on the bureau. It was a terrible error to have refused him, a miscalculation. "You've got to learn to say no," her housemates had told her back in college, but they were talking about all the strangers whose voices they heard through her bedroom door, not Carl, who was slowly making her feel like she could love a man who knew her.

He was on his feet now, taking her elbow and inching her toward the bed. He spent the night apologizing for various perceived infractions, wondering if she was pregnant, and making love to her from the front. In the morning Mrs. Riordan brought them a breakfast tray filled with black-and-white pudding, eggs sunny-side up, and tomatoes silken with grease from the frying pan. At the center of the tray—propped against two mugs of steaming tea—was a telegram, something Shayna had never before seen. A smile escaped Carl as his eyes passed over it: READ OF YOUR WEDDING STOP WANT TO THROTTLE YOU FOR NOT TELLING US STOP WANT TO APOLOGIZE FOR BOOK STOP WANT TO KISS YOUR LOVELY BRIDE.

it was decided that now that he was a married man, Carl would learn to drive. Mother, as Mrs. Meara instructed Shayna to call her when they hugged at Dublin airport, would have to do the teaching. "I don't have my license," Niall explained as he drove them all home in a taupe Peugeot, and there was no laughter from the others to indicate that this wasn't true.

Shayna sat beside Carl in the back seat of the car, staring

at the back of her father-in-law's head. There was a bald spot at the center of it, and a crown of soft brown hair decorating the rim. Because Niall was tall, he drove with his head tilted slightly downward so as to avoid bumping the vinyl ceiling. Over the course of the ride Shayna met his eyes twice in the rearview mirror, each time catching the beginnings of his smile before she quickly turned away.

Mother was heavy and raven-haired like Carl. She wore a silky tank top revealing beautiful, poreless skin at the nape of her neck, and perspired discreetly under her arms. She too was losing her hair, but remained stylishly coiffed that afternoon with the help of ornamental combs and a light spray. "What's your hurry?" she demanded repeatedly of Niall, and he answered her with polite deceleration.

The Mearas lived in south Dublin, in a large brick row house across from the sea. It was a wealthy area, with many of the homes boasting the colorful Georgian doors Shayna had seen on postcards at the airport, and good-sized gardens both in front and at the back. The driveway Niall pulled into already held a Mercedes, and he didn't seem bothered by the light tap he gave its bumper before turning off the Peugeot. "We won't stay long," Carl suddenly warned his parents.

Once inside the house they separated, embarrassed. Mother headed for the kitchen, which smelled of roasting meat, and Niall for the living room directly off the foyer. Neither of them seemed to want to watch Carl and Shayna ascend the stairs together, Carl's hand resting purposefully on Shayna's bottom.

They stayed in his old bedroom, located directly above the living room and with a full ocean view. Carl got behind the chiffon drapes and opened the tall windows, then swore bitterly at the twin beds his mother had made up. The walls were decorated with various paintings of Niall—some abstract, some realistic—and carefully Carl took all of these down, leaning them against the wall facing inward.

He unzipped himself then and sat down on an overstuffed chair in the corner, asking Shayna to come sit with him. She found him juvenile, romantic. She appreciated both his initiative and the regularity of his advances. It was becoming addictive, the gentle claim he had laid to her, not having to work so hard to belong to someone else.

Carl's driving lessons took him and mother away from the house several afternoons a week. Shayna stayed behind as a favor to Carl, who confessed he was embarrassed that she already had her license. "I wouldn't laugh at you," she assured him, and he said he knew that, but didn't want to take any unnecessary chances.

Across the road, Shayna continued the walks along the coast she and Carl had begun on their honeymoon, mindful of Mother's edict that Niall wrote during the day and should not be engaged in conversation, not even if he were to provide an opening remark. She walked to the port, where ferries from England docked and departed, noting the silence with which people left the country, the noise upon their return. She waved to strangers as they pulled away, and was even recognized on a couple of occasions as the Yank who had captured Carl Meara. "Will you take a photo?" people asked her, chuckling at how she held out her hand for their cameras instead of joining them for the pose.

Sometimes she ventured inland, buying treats along the way from sandwich shops with enticing window displays, corner markets selling candy bars from England. If her eyes happened to be bigger than her stomach on any given day, she would leave the untouched remainders outside the door of Niall's third-floor study: a sweet cheese bagel from a tiny Jewish bakery, a hunk of soda bread and a peeled tangerine on a tray.

He never mentioned her gifts at dinner. Instead, they all sat together at one end of a long, rectangular table in the dining room, Mother and Carl recounting the adventures of their travels: curvy back roads through County Wicklow, one-way bridges, sheep crossings requiring patience and a true ease with one's clutch. They told about an old farmer who leaned into the car to give them directions, flies swarming about his head and back; an American hitchhiker who spoke perfect Irish.

"When are you going to start showing this girl around?" Niall demanded one evening. He had just finished soaking up the last of his bloody roast beef with a heel of bread, and now punctuated his question by tossing a white serviette on the table.

"First of all," Carl began slowly, preparing to swallow a mouthful of food, "she's not a girl. By no means is she a girl."

"Semantics," Mother said to Shayna, looking to gather consensus.

"Second of all," Carl continued, "don't even think of suggesting I am neglecting my wife. I can assure you, my wife does not feel neglected." He looked to Shayna for confirmation, but she was too embarrassed to answer, worried he was referring to the sexual component of their relationship.

"All right, all right," Niall said. "Don't get your knickers in a twist."

"And third of all, you should consider yourselves bloody lucky we're here at all."

"Now, hold on just one second!" Mother said, throwing her napkin on the table as well. "What about our excursions? Don't you lump me in with that man." She gestured loosely toward Niall.

"But we do consider ourselves lucky," Niall said quickly, turning first to Carl, then Shayna. "We consider ourselves very lucky. You must know that."

"Naturally," Mother said to no one in particular.

Carl tore into a multigrain roll. "I'll show her around when I get my license," he concluded. "So's I can leave the likes of you two at home."

Niall laughed, followed by Carl, and a reluctant Mother.

"Would you look at that one," Niall said, noting Shayna's own grin. "Silent as the grave, she is."

He winked at her, and she fixed her gaze nervously on the wineglass beside her plate. If she felt neglected it was only by him. That he would not come out of his room.

Carl did not show Shayna around after getting his license. Instead, he explained to her that touring the countryside with his mother had led him to conclude he could never return to a land so vile as England, and that somehow he would have to make his own way at home. He proceeded to rehang all the paintings of his father in their bedroom—done by various artist friends—then sit on the twin beds he had pushed together and study each of them intently, trying to pick a style he felt most capable of emulating. He had not previously taken art classes, but was certain some kind of creative gene must run through him, and that the fine arts were as good a place as any to try to locate it.

At first he attempted nude portraits of Shayna, but had difficulty with the human form and could not restrain himself from interacting with his subject. Landscapes were easier, but only when she was not lying lazily beside him in the grass, her summer clothing shifting this way and that. He feared he would have to do this alone, he told her, and suggested that since they had settled on staying, Shayna should start searching for her own talent. She had sewn buttons and tears in his clothing quite impressively, Carl offered, so why not apprentice herself with a seamstress, or even a costume designer at the Abbey? She agreed this was a good idea and dressed herself one morning to look professional, though she never made it out the door. As she was gathering her résumé in the bedroom, Niall summoned her from the third floor, gave her a typing test, and immediately hired her as his secretary.

He had begun a new book about a beautiful mute who falls in love with a concert violinist. He wrote everything out in longhand on yellow legal pads, and it was Shayna's job as his secretary to type this into his computer, correcting any spelling or grammatical errors she found along the way. She found none.

They worked together in his office on the third floor, she at a table facing the paneled back wall, he at a desk overlooking the sea. Because they sat with their backs to each other she could not see him, and so often worried where his eyes fell in those moments when the scratch of his fountain pen subsided. She began sitting up straighter in her chair and, in the mornings, meticulously styling the hair at the back of her head.

Sometimes Niall laughed covetously over what he had written; other times he cursed his inactivity lyrically, poetically, as if to prove he had not lost all command of language. Occasionally he would write very, very quickly, and these passages were always the most difficult for Shayna to transcribe the following day. Even in her privileged position as his secretary, she continued to find his work dull.

They broke for lunch daily at one. At first she retreated to her bedroom, leaving Niall to eat with Mother in the kitchen. Shayna used this time to examine any new work Carl had left behind, with notes attached, such as "Credible resemblance to poplar?" or "Superfluous orange? Please advise." He often left the house before dawn to take advantage of the morning light, which he described as "fundamental" and "shattering." He felt similarly about sunset and so rarely returned home before eight or nine o'clock. Then, wanting to make up for lost time, he kept Shayna in bed with him for the rest of the evening, encouraging her not to stifle her noises, particularly when he had a sense of Niall in the living room below, reading one of his literary journals from America.

Then one afternoon, after returning to the office, Niall asked Shayna, "Is there some reason you won't join Mother and me for lunch?"

The answer was that Shayna felt Mother was on to her; understood that her daughter-in-law was capable of loving her son and coveting her husband, all in one breath.

"I'm asking you a direct question, Shayna," Niall said, impatient. "Maybe Carl prefers the silent type, but I'm perfectly happy to have you exhibit symptoms of a personality."

"I have an answer," she said dimly, looking around the room at more glaring portraits of him, framed book jackets, the antique bric-a-brac Mother must have had a hand in. They were both standing by their respective chairs, she and Niall, and now he sat down in his, eyes still pinned on her. Finally she told him she was trying to give him and Mother some time alone.

He laughed. "Do Mother and I seem like we need time alone? I don't think so. Really, Shayna. All those days out there"—he gestured toward his window and the shore beyond—"pacing the country and looking positively enlightened, and this is the dreck you're storing upstairs?" He tapped the side of his head with his index finger.

She cried instantly, which seemed to make him happy. "Here," he said, removing a kerchief from his corduroy pants pocket. "These are Mother's idea. I'm supposed to offer them to ladies in distress."

Shayna came forward and took the pressed linen cloth from him.

"Are you in distress?" he asked her.

She blew her nose.

"Who taught you to be quiet?" he said.

"I did," she said.

"That's a lie," he said, and he picked up his yellow pad and began scribbling.

The next day she followed him downstairs for lunch. Mother said it was delightful to see Shayna, then spoke to Niall in Irish for the better part of an hour. Later, back in his office, he said he would be happy to translate every word if Shayna thought she had any interest in Mother's recollection of a phone call with her eye doctor.

"Will Mother's vision be all right?" Shayna asked Niall, and he laughed, declaring her manners "novel."

More and more, Shayna spoke. She told Niall about the night she first met Carl, how he had refused to take off his jacket, saying it was the only thing protecting Shayna from his stomach. She remembered a small, green leaf in his hair. She even talked a little about college, and the anthropology teacher who had called Shayna her most promising student in years.

"Do you read my books?" Niall asked.

"No," she said plainly, causing him infinite delight.

He asked her other questions that she could not answer: Why don't your parents ever call here? Does my son plan to take you out of this house? Where did you get that scar on your back? Who taught you to be quiet?

Unlikely sounds were beginning to emanate from his study, they both knew: a ballet of office chairs squeaking across planked floors, the unbecoming giggles of a grown man, loud conspicuous silences during which nothing— neither Niall's fountain pen, nor Shayna's manicured nails across the keyboard—moved. One day Mother took a broom handle to the ceiling below them, like a disgruntled neighbor too lazy—or afraid—to make the trip upstairs. "Make some noise, will you, so I know you're still alive!" she demanded. She was right to disturb them. Though nothing official had yet taken place, they had begun contemplating zippers, buttons, hooks and eyes. Unabashed stares passed between them. With increasing frequency, they spent their afternoons in the same chair.

Carl took Shayna to a pub in town one night to show her off to his old college mates. She wore a black summer dress and he a fine linen shirt given to him by Mother, who had recently put herself in charge of his new style. For painting had somehow caused Carl to lose weight—had given him a marvelous tan—and friends and strangers alike told him what a handsome figure he cut.

Shayna had previously talked some politics with Niall, and took the opportunity that night to repeat much of what he believed to Carl's friends, who instantly pronounced her a genius. Later, having missed the last bus, Carl led her inside the stone walls of Trinity College and onto a green littered with several anonymous couples. There, with very little moon to expose them, they performed something so expert and efficient, it would appear not to have happened at all.

During the two-hour walk home, Shayna took the opportunity to reveal to Carl that she believed him to be talented, and he said it had to be true, didn't it, since he had never once heard her compliment anyone before. When they arrived at the house, he had no urge to go inside. "Sit with me on the beach," he begged her, tugging lightly at the fabric of her dress. "I like the sound of your voice."

They stayed out all night, discussing his paintings, his father's new book, their recent cessation of any contraception. They watched the sun come up and Carl described the different shades of orange and yellow passing over Shayna's face, telling her exactly how much yellow, red, and white it would take to re-create from a tube. "Do you like Dublin?" he asked her hopefully. She nodded and reminded him of something one of his friends had insisted upon earlier that night, that you couldn't walk through the city center without running into someone you knew. "I want to stay here until that happens to me," she said.

At a little after six, Niall brought them mugs of tea and asked how his son planned to paint that day, having had no rest the night before. Carl assured him it could be done and left immediately to get cleaned up. Niall, still standing, claimed the vacant spot beside Shayna, and she cuffed an arm around his ankle. "And how about you?" he asked her, looking down. "How do you plan to be my secretary today?"

But she was not his secretary. He had never once paid her, and there had not been work for days.

An hour later mother had French toast sizzling on the griddle, and the four of them ate together at the round, mosaic-topped kitchen table. Mother had recently hung many of Carl's paintings in the living room in anticipation of a party she had planned for that evening. It was an occasion both for Carl to reacquaint himself with his parents' artist friends and for Mother to ascertain whether or not his talent was too big for Dublin. On this point Niall, who was careful to agree that Carl's talent was indeed large, begged to differ, saying an Irishman with talent belonged strictly to Ireland. Of course, of course, Mother agreed, but how about some formal training in Florence or Paris first? Paris, after all, where Shayna could be closer to her father.

Now Mother wanted to know everyone's plans for the day, saying her caterer and the maid would not appreciate stragglers underfoot. "I'm painting," Carl said, downing his third cup of tea.

"We're writing," Niall said, nodding toward Shayna.

Mother, who was still wearing her cooking apron, raised an eyebrow. "Is that so, missus? You're a writer now, too?"

Shayna shook her head.

"Of course not," Mother said. "You're the muse, I gather. You *inspire*."

"Does she inspire you, Da?" Carl asked his father.

"She types," Niall said. "She's a brilliant typist, and she catches all my mistakes. If that isn't inspiration, I don't know what is."

"Then I guess you don't know what is," Carl said, pushing his chair away from the table.

"She's quiet anyway," Mother said warily.

"No, she's not," Carl and Niall said at the same time, and it was embarrassing to them all that Shayna should have become the center of attention.

Later in his study, Niall and Shayna stood side by side looking out the window at the shore. The water was gray from nearby harbor traffic but the sun shone down on it nonetheless, as if to assure them that even the polluted was worthy of a little beauty.

All at once Shayna's fatigue struck, and she leaned into Niall, who made no immediate move for her in return. Instead he spoke quietly, asking which pub she had gone to the night before, how she had found Carl's mates, did she know she still carried the sea in her hair? She answered him carefully, thoroughly, relieved that she was capable of doing so after her silence at breakfast. When he too was satisfied that the girl he liked best had not vanished, he suggested they get out of Mother's way and go swimming. Did she know how, he wondered? Did she have togs, healthy lungs, the appropriate amount of body fat to protect her from the chill of the Irish Sea? She let him pinch her waist gently, then hug her, then pull her onto his lap. There he petted and kissed her, murmuring over how soft she was, how tidily she fit across his legs. She could feel him beneath her but he seemed disinterested in garnering any personal attention, catching her wrist as she reached for his trousers. "Never mind that," he whispered, as if he had become a nuisance to himself, as if right and wrong still existed between them.

The Peugeot curved along the Vico Road, bordered on one side by rocky cliffs leading down to the sea, and on the other by higher cliffs into which pale, glass-fronted homes were intermittently pressed. At the top of a rise, Niall pulled onto the shoulder beside a pea-green sign reading NO SWIMMING. The wind forced tall weeds against his and Shayna's bare legs as they stepped from the car, and flattened their T-shirts against their chests. "Here?" she asked him, unsure of how they would make their way down to the water, while Niall offered his hand.

They helped each other over a waist-high concrete barrier once designed to keep people from irradiating themselves in the contaminated sea (though Niall assured Shayna the danger had long since passed), and descended rocks so civilized as to hint at being stairs. They dug the heels of their tennis shoes into slippery patches of peat, braved the odd crevasse, and, when all else failed, encouraged each other to jump. Always Niall went first, testing each step, instructing Shayna on how to avoid the scratches and bruises he had sustained at the helm. They traveled too slowly, too cautiously. It was a journey fraught with the minor yet repeated heartache of having to drop hands each time the terrain forced them more than an arm's length apart.

At last they reached a plateau littered with towels, apple cores, and a few sleeping sunbathers. To their right was a small cave painted thick with graffiti—a changing room, Niall informed Shayna—while farther below, an old metal diving board jutted out over water so wrongfully green that surely it must still hold chemicals.

"Niall Meara!" a man with a silver schnauzer called out.

Niall waved but did not approach the man. "Do you know him?" Shayna asked.

He shrugged and dropped her hand. "It's possible."

On a nearby rock, they laid out the towels they had been carrying around their necks. Niall stripped down to a yellow Speedo with a small black emblem, then removed a pair of doughy-looking plugs from his shorts and stuffed them in his ears.

"Take them out," Shayna said, worried he would not be able to hear her should she decide to speak, and after briefly considering this request, he did.

Shayna's own swimsuit was a plain black one-piece with thin straps that crisscrossed in the back. Before meeting Carl she had swum almost every day at an indoor pool in London, dizzying herself both from exercise and routine collisions with the concrete at either end of her lane.

"There it is," Niall said, pointing. "That's where we're headed." Shayna followed his index finger out across the water until she saw the peninsula, a cliff crumbling bit by bit into the sea. "Think you can make it?" he asked.

She nodded. It was no more than an hour's swim away.

"Mother never had any trouble," he said.

"What's Mother's name?" Shayna asked.

Niall looked at her, confused. "Kathleen," he said, turning back to the peninsula now, scanning it from left to right as he would a line of text. "Kathleen Sleeth," he added.

"Oh," she said.

"My God," he said, shaking his head sadly as he walked off toward the diving board. "I'd nearly forgotten."

Once there he tested the spring, shook his arms out like a competitor, and reached down to touch his hands to his toes. There was not a wrinkle on him, Shayna noted, though he was easily sixty. The casual atrophy of his muscles hinted gracefully at his former physique. Shayna couldn't see the bathers beneath him, but their calls of *Niall Meara! Brace yourself, Niall Meara! The water's bloody freezing!* rang in clearly at the shore.

He looked back at her once before executing a clean dive. Shayna then made her way toward a mossy rock beneath the diving board from which she planned to push off, all the while listening to scattered applause for Niall's performance. When she reached the rock, she saw him treading water near a small group of young women. "What's your latest book about then?" one of them asked him. She pronounced *book* to rhyme with *spook*.

"It's a romance," Niall told her, fixing his gaze on Shayna, who had yet to submerge herself. "Something for the ladies."

"Well, that's grand," the woman said, following Niall's eyes to the shore when he failed to make polite eye contact with her.

"My daughter-in-law," he explained.

The woman nodded, then quickly rejoined her friends. Niall began swimming backward then, away from the shore, away from Shayna. She panicked and quickly thrust herself forward into the water.

It was very, very cold. Immediately Shayna felt injured and in need of medical care, but she pushed on toward Niall, who was putting greater and greater distance between them. She thought of the parents in the swimming pool in London, always moving backward through the water with their arms extended, in an effort to get their kids to swim just a little bit farther. And soon she began to feel grateful, for her desperate strokes had begun to warm first her extremities, then the cushy parts of her that were less temperature sensitive. She had still not caught up to Niall, but was satisfied to have at least cut his lead.

All the while he kept his eyes on her as they swam, smiling sometimes, or spouting water from his lips. Shayna alternated strokes, showing off, silently daring him not to compliment her abilities when they reached the peninsula. Fish slithered between her feet and she did not scream. Her swimsuit abandoned her in several places, and she didn't bother to fix it.

Niall reached the shore first, but by the time he had calculated the sequence of rocks that would lead them out of the water, Shayna was beside him, pinching mucus from her nose. "Most impressive," he told her before heaving himself onto land. He then turned and offered his hand, pulling her up with a rush of ocean. It was afternoon and she understood they would find a place to be private.

Niall led Shayna carefully over fallen boulders, continuing to warn her that he had just stubbed his toe, or to mind any particularly large gaps. They traveled partway up the jagged ramp of the cliff, then down again into a hollow of geometric stone, a place where the sun still reached, but not likely the human eye. It was clearly a popular place—filled with bottles, cans, wrappers, cigarette butts, used condoms— and Niall breathed a sigh of relief to find it empty. He declared with utter certainty that the closest person to them right now was at least an hour away.

Here, on a flat rock made smooth by previous visitors— including, Shayna supposed, Niall and Mother—he was comfortable kissing her, holding her in his lap, rearranging her bathing suit so that it covered the delicate parts of her. "No," she said, not wanting to be covered, but he insisted, and she knew this was as close as he would allow himself to get.

Later he found the scar on her shoulder, the one her summer dresses sometimes revealed: a slim, raised sickle. "Who made this?" he asked again, running his fingers over it carefully. "I did," she said, and before he could tell her she was lying, she described an aftermath on a fraternity-room floor, a broken bottle she had rolled onto as she patted the rug for her blouse.

They sat together for a long time after that, until their swimsuits dried and their skin temperatures elevated. Beneath her, Niall hardened and softened, and she felt unsure of who she was if she wasn't there to relieve him. But she did not try, instead studying him closely: the sleepy eyes, the slightly bar-reled chest, the old-man fingernails splayed across her legs.

As the sun began its descent into the west, Niall jerked awake. "I can't go back in," he suddenly confessed to her, his ears alert to the encroaching tide. "I've lost my tolerance and I can't go back in." He was calm again in an instant, but for the dark moment that had just passed she whispered assur-ances of warm water, and kissed him everywhere she could think that was decent.

On the Occasion of my Ruination

it was summer, as i suppose it tended to be. i was living with my mother, who had taken a job as a secretary with the city's minor league baseball team. She was a high school teacher by trade, so money was nonexistent during the summer months. For the rest of the year, she complained about how much she hated teenagers.

I had enrolled in community college after graduating high school, then dropped out after the first year to work. Now, a year after dropping out, I was on the verge of leaving home for a state school a couple of hours away. I had found a room with an attached porch in a house with three other transfers, and my father had reluctantly agreed to pay rent. He and my mother had been divorced for several years, and he had a lot of concerns about the two of us living high on the hog. "What kind of mansion are we talking about here?" he asked me, and I assured him it was really just an old, sagging house with an attached porch.

But I still had three weeks left of work at the mall, in a lingerie store called Angelina's Whisper, a rip-off of Victoria's Secret. All the same, if you worked at Angelina's, the other mall employees seemed to think you were really something— that you had a lot of sex, that your underpants were always wet, that your skirt slid across your ass so smoothly because you were wearing something satiny underneath. Maybe this was true of my co-workers, Evelyn and Mina, but I wasn't interested in lingerie. I tried it on once and it made me look like an idiot.

In particular, the guys at the pizza place across from Angelina's seemed to pay a lot of attention to us. They flirted more with Evelyn and Mina, who were both married and knew what they were doing, but also with me sometimes, if the mood struck them. I wasn't all that good at flirting. Renaldo, who owned the pizza place, told me I should smile more—that my smile was *bella,* and that boys no like no smile. So I would smile at him and he'd say, "Thatsa good!" which I didn't get, since when I duplicated the smile at home in the mirror I thought I looked tense and miserable. One day I said, "Renaldo, isn't it possible that a person who isn't smiling could feel fine on the inside?" He shook his head, and seemed extremely disappointed in me.

Every day we went to the pizza shop for coffee, Coke, pizza, and salads. Evelyn and Mina flirted with Renaldo and his son Bert, while I went after the new part-time guy who didn't look Italian at all. He had blond hair and icy green eyes that were spaced a little too far apart. He was well-built, and I pitied him the plastic food-handling gloves that cut off the circulation in his meaty hands. Whenever he waited on me, he removed them and handled my food personally, which I took to be a sign of intimacy. Though Evelyn and Mina agreed he was handsome, they ignored him out of respect for me, as I had set my sights on losing my virginity to him before heading off to school.

"I just saw your boyfriend," Evelyn said one afternoon, returning from the pizza place with a cup of coffee. She was short and slim, though when she looked in the mirror, seemed only to see a big butt. "I told him you wanted him," she added solemnly.

"You did not," I said. We were standing behind a glass display case, on top of which sat the cash register and the pale blue tissue paper we used to wrap purchases.

She laughed. "Of course I didn't."

Part of me wished she had been serious. "So what do I do?" I said. "How do I get him to ask me out?"

She shrugged. "Just keep going over there, I guess."

Mina, who had been straightening the racks, came over carrying a black teddy on a hanger. She was stout and had long brown hair she vowed never to cut. "What do you think?" she asked us, holding the teddy up in front of her.

"Cute," Evelyn said, then turned her attention to a list of

markdowns we planned to tackle that afternoon. Mina had recently lost favor with Evelyn after attending a party at Evelyn's house and showing off how her husband could remove her bra through her shirt-sleeve. "I must've accidentally sent out the wrong invitations," Evelyn had grumbled the next day. *"You're invited to an orgy!"*

But Mina was oblivious. She took the teddy into the back room, where we hid things we didn't want the customers to lay their hands on.

"Okay," I said finally. "I'll go over there and get a Coke." I opened my purse and took out my wallet.

"Ask him his name!" Evelyn called after me as I made my way past the racks of teddies and bustiers, the tables stacked with jewel-toned underwear and velvet slippers.

Directly in front of me, as i entered the mall, was the shoe repairman. He was a tough-looking guy who had a crush on Evelyn, and to whom she brought all manner of pumps, whether or not they needed fixing. Her visits to him increased when she and her husband were fighting, though she denied any emotional attachment on her part. To the right of the shoe repair was the toy store. I had had a brief fling with one of the sales associates there, Doug, in July, but ultimately it had come to nothing. It seemed to Evelyn that he must be gay, and that this was why he had broken it off with me. She had a lot of faith in me, Evelyn did, so I said nothing about having called Doug incessantly once it was over, crying and howling even though he told me to leave him alone.

To the left, on the other side of the shoe repair, was the

pizza place. It was an old mall, and so far no one had taken the time to establish a food court; there was just Renaldo's Pizzeria and a sub shop farther down. As I approached the service counter, which faced onto the mall, I saw Green Eyes waiting on someone at a second counter inside the restaurant. I waited patiently for him, playing with the snap on my wallet. Green Eyes saw me but acted like he didn't. This was just another aspect of our intimacy; he would wait on everyone else in line before me so that at last we could be alone.

Renaldo popped out of the kitchen for a moment and told me to smile, but I ignored him. He went back in and as the door swung open, I caught a glimpse of Bert, wearing a white paper hat and stretching out pizza dough with two fists. He winked at me and I winked back, which was probably not what Evelyn would've done, though Mina might have.

"Hey," Green Eyes said, ripping off his food-service gloves. His fingers were blue and he kneaded invisible dough to get the blood flowing again. I watched him and thought that if we ever went on a date, I'd want him to dress exactly like this: khakis, a white T-shirt, and a white apron around his neck.

"Hi," I said.

He turned his body sideways to the counter and leaned toward me on one elbow. We were very intimate now. He touched my wallet. "What can I get you?" he asked.

I said he could get me a Coke. He nodded, but made no move for the drink machine.

"You like working over there?" he asked me, glancing toward Angelina's.

I shrugged. I had no idea how to act with men. From what I could gather you were supposed to be alternately rude and mocking. Never nice. "Yes," I said, managing something closer to shell-shocked.

"Make you horny?" he asked.

I laughed. You were definitely supposed to laugh a lot. "No!" And protest loudly.

"Really?" he said. He seemed sincere.

I was at a loss. "It would make me horny if it was Victoria's Secret," I said finally.

He laughed. "Yeah, well. Either one works for me."

"Could I get that Coke?" I said, suddenly hitting my stride.

He went and got me a Coke. I paid him and he tickled my palm with his fingers as he returned my change. "What's your name?" he asked.

"Gilda," I said.

He nodded.

"What's yours?"

"I'm Jonathan," he said. Then he added, "I'm thinking of asking you out. I'll let you know what I decide."

As I had proven with Doug, I was not so easily thrown off the scent. "Just hurry up," I told him, zipping my change purse shut. "I leave for college at the end of the month."

At home that night, i told my mother about Jonathan. We were sitting at the kitchen table, eating cereal for dinner. "He's after me," I said casually. Never in my life had I discussed boys with her, probably because there had been so few to discuss.

My mother, who had had a bouncy Dorothy Hamill haircut since the 1976 Olympics, shrugged her shoulders. Her own boyfriend, Roscoe, was twenty years older than she was. She had met him through a single-parent group, and had selected him as her steady because he was the thinnest man there. Roscoe had several grown children who seemed to like my mother better than him, and he owned a sailboat, which had capsized earlier that summer. My mother, an avid swimmer, had had to save his life, though she seemed irritated about this. In her diary she confessed that he was impotent.

Now she pushed her cereal bowl aside, a few bloated Puffed Rice drifting aimlessly in the gray milk. "Well," she said, "I guess it's nice to feel wanted."

I nodded confidently. "Oh yeah." I was eating Cap'n Crunch, which represented adulthood to me, as I had bought it with my own money. My mother didn't believe in sugar cereals.

She lit a cigarette and exhaled up toward the globe light that hung from the ceiling. In a fit of courage, I grabbed the pack of Kools and lit one myself. My mother laughed dismissively. "You don't smoke," she said.

"Sure I do," I said. "Watch." I then demonstrated my inability to blow smoke rings, though clearly I could inhale without choking.

"I stand corrected," my mother said at last. She herself

blew a perfect smoke ring, then invited me to feel free to smoke in the house. "No use sneaking around," she told me.

I felt we had solidified something in that moment—we had agreed that I was an adult with my cereal, my prospective boyfriend, and finally my vice. I don't know if my mother knew I was still a virgin; frankly, I don't think she gave it a second thought. In the sixties, she had started a fund for women to obtain safe abortions. She was liberal in that way; sugar cereals made a greater impression on her than sex. I was fortunate that she had passed some of this attitude on to me, though I had ultimately failed to become promiscuous. Instead I was halting and quiet, with a wit that only Evelyn really knew about. It was this highly ineffective combination of character traits—insecurity and sexual liberation—that had left me "intact," as Mina called it, at the ripe old age of nineteen.

That night my mother, Roscoe, and I all went to see our hometown team play ball. My mother got free tickets for all the games, and they weren't nosebleed seats either. Tonight we sat behind home plate, Roscoe on the aisle, since the medicine he took for his heart made him pee a lot. I caught a foul ball with my old softball glove and, at the end of the game, had the guy who hit it autograph it to Jonathan.

it was slow at Angelina's the next day, so we all joked around with the baseball, stuffing it down our shirts and walking around like we were really something, even though we were lopsided. "Just keep your bra on," Evelyn warned Mina as she removed the baseball from beneath her blouse, and I could tell all had been forgiven concerning the party.

I took the ball from Mina and passed it back and forth between my hands. "It's warm," I said.

Evelyn said, "Gross!" She didn't like anything to escape from her person, or to hear about how it had escaped from somebody else's: no sounds, no fluids, no smells, no temperatures. I think she wished she were invisible. Often I wanted to tell her she looked pretty, but I knew it would only make her mad.

"You gonna give Jonathan the ball?" Mina asked me. She winked.

I looked at Evelyn. "Do you think I should?"

She shrugged. "I can't tell you what to do."

"I'll give it to him," Mina offered. "I'll point out the autograph and tell him it's from you."

"Excuse me!" Evelyn said. "She's about to leave for college, not high school. She has to give it to him herself."

"So you *would* give it to him," I concluded, though it came out more like a question.

Mina thought it over and said, "You know what? Yes!"

I wasn't talking to her and we all knew it, though no one said anything.

Finally Evelyn said, "It's up to you."

"But what would you do if you were me?" I pressed her.

"Give it to the shoe guy," Mina said.

Evelyn ignored her. "What have you got to lose?" she said.

We all laughed then, three women in the business of sex.

i carried the baseball in my purse. At the pizza place, Jonathan had a line of customers three people deep. I waited a few minutes, then, when it seemed to be taking too long, made a move to leave. But Jonathan saw me and called out, "Wait! Gilda! It'll only be a few more minutes." The people in line turned around to look at me, and I smiled. When they were facing the counter again, Jonathan announced, "I'm thinking of asking her out. I've just about decided." He winked at me then, and I mumbled—quite involuntarily—"Idiot." The woman in front of me, who was carrying a bag from the half-price shoe store, heard this and told me, "Follow your instincts. My son goes to high school with him and I'm telling you, he runs with a *fast* crowd."

Fast I needed. It was the high school part that surprised me. I thanked her for the advice nonetheless.

When it was my turn to order—when Jonathan had stripped off his plastic gloves and taken his sideways, leaning posture against the counter—I said, "So you're in high school."

He turned red.

"What grade?" I asked.

He straightened up and fetched me a drink from the machine. "I'll be a junior this year," he said.

"So, a sophomore," I said, mulling it over.

"No," he corrected me. "A junior."

"Until school starts, you're technically a sophomore." I had just made that up, but he seemed to believe it.

"So?" he said, giving me change for my drink. He always undercharged me about twenty cents.

I shrugged. "It's cute."

He leaned in again, bringing his face close to mine. "Hey," he said, very softly, as if neither of us was wearing clothes. "The thing is, I was lying to those people. I've already decided. I decided a long time ago. I want to take you out."

I thought about the baseball in my purse. It seemed all wrong now.

"I want to take you out before you leave for college," he persisted. Then he picked up my Coke, which had a clear straw sticking out of it, and took a sip. He handed it back to me and, when I wouldn't take it, set it down on the counter. "If you can drink from this, you can sure as hell kiss me, right?"

"Get me another one," I demanded. He was really bringing out the best in me.

"No," he said, his breath oddly fruity.

We exchanged phone numbers then, and agreed he would pick me up at seven-thirty that night.

When Jonathan arrived at my house, i was waiting on the front steps in a black tubular skirt and an army surplus V-neck—the lowest-cut T-shirt I owned. Underneath I wore a bra from Angelina's that Evelyn and Mina had insisted I buy in order to improve my *décolletage,* as Mina called it. As much as I had bucked against this purchase, I couldn't keep from looking down and admiring its astounding effect. My hair, a nondescript brown, was apparently the envy of many of Angelina's customers due to its curl. "Is that natural?" they'd ask me. When I nodded my head they'd say, "I hate you," then quickly pat my hand to reassure me this wasn't true. Otherwise, I didn't seem to have anything anyone else wanted. Or if I did, they hadn't mentioned it.

"I would've rung your doorbell," Jonathan said once I had let myself into his car. I ignored him and made a sophisticated production of locating the seat belt in a Buick (my mother always bought foreign). The truth was, I'd never been picked up for a date before and wasn't exactly sure of where to wait. Also, my mother was out having dinner with Roscoe, and I worried that without her as chaperone, I'd begin the date backward and lose my virginity in the first five minutes. Technically, I felt there was nothing wrong with this. But there was something of the john in me that night. I wanted to pretend for at least a little while that I didn't know how the evening was going to turn out. "It's okay," I said finally, clicking my buckle in place. "The house is a mess."

I watched Jonathan as he backed out of my gravel driveway, disappointed in his choice of ensemble: a sporty polo shirt and pleated, pressed trousers. At last I could see the high-schooler in him, when it was really the greasy mall worker I wanted. But there was some comfort to be taken from the glare he shot me when I laughed at the orange fuzzy dice hanging from his rearview mirror. He popped the song "Feel Like Makin' Love" into his cassette deck, and that wasn't a joke either. Jonathan was as serious tonight as he had ever been at the pizza place. I suspected he really did feel like making love.

"So," I said, raising my voice above Bad Company, "you're still in high school?"

"Could you stop bringing that up?" Jonathan asked me.

"Sorry," I said. It was just that I didn't have anything else on him, and I really felt I needed the upper hand.

We were passing through the suburbs now, heading for the city, where any self-respecting date would take place. Silently I cursed all the chain restaurants and prefab banks, though I had not known until that particular moment that I even resented them.

"My parents aren't home this weekend," Jonathan offered.

"Oh yeah?" I said.

"Yeah," he said.

He drove like someone who had just gotten his driver's license and was in no hurry to lose it, keeping his hands strictly at ten and two on the wheel and glancing my way only when he hit a stoplight. His old Skylark was slightly jacked up in the back, and I wondered when he would loosen up and start driving it accordingly. At the same time, he clearly wasn't afraid of the road. It hit me then that we drove somewhat similarly, and might've shared the same driver's ed teacher in school. I opened my mouth to ask him about this, then remembered my promise to keep quiet on the subject.

"What?" Jonathan asked me.

"Nothing," I said, the beginning of my question still hanging in the air.

He shrugged. "Must've been something."

"It was," I confirmed.

He laughed. "So what do you want to do tonight? Where do you want to go?"

"We'll see the new James Bond movie." Suddenly I had all the confidence of a drunk, except I was sober.

He nodded. Then without looking at me he said, "You look really nice tonight. Even sexier than at work."

"Thanks," I said. "To be honest, I actually prefer your work clothes on you."

He couldn't believe this. He pulled into an empty bank parking lot, looked down at himself, and said, "For real?"

"Let's go back to your house so you can change," I suggested, suddenly thrilled at the prospect of this.

"You're kidding or you're serious?" he asked me.

"Serious," I said. "How far is it?"

He smiled and turned the car around. "Not that far." He was excited, too, I could tell.

Jonathan lived in a development of two-story ranch houses that I imagined were all pastel-colored in daylight. At night they only looked to be varying shades of white. "I'll wait here," I said, when he pulled up in front of his place. Again I feared losing control of myself while alone with him in a space larger than the front seat of his car.

"Come in and watch me change," he said, cutting the engine and lowering his voice.

"Nah," I said.

He didn't move. He was staring at me, and this was making me a little bit shy. I kept my eyes glued to the street in front of me, Persimmon Place. "You're really—" he began, but he didn't finish. He started over again and said, "I'm feeling really lucky to be here with you."

"Why?" I asked. "I thought you had to think so hard about asking me out."

Jonathan laughed. "That was Renaldo's idea," he said. "Renaldo said he could tell you wanted me, and to take things nice and slow."

"Meanwhile, I leave for college at the end of the month," I reminded him.

He struck his forehead with the palm of his hand. "Fucking Renaldo!" he said. Then he said, "Be right back."

While he was gone I decided I loved him. I envisioned the two of us on my attached back porch at college, where I might even think about putting my bed. Me with a boyfriend from home! He would come and my roommates would tease me about robbing the cradle, though secretly they would covet him. Jonathan might give them the once-over, but because they would all have straight hair and bras that could not perform miracles, he would never succumb. And the more Jonathan saw of the world, the more his focus upon me would narrow, until finally, in an odd twist of fate, I would suddenly become traditional and marry the first man I had slept with.

He emerged from the house moments later in a snug

white T-shirt, frayed khakis, and a pair of no-frills basketball shoes. When he got in the car, I mussed his blond hair until he was the picture of an employee.

"You want a slice of pizza?" he asked me.

We laughed as he started the car, and I rewound the tape to the beginning.

We got to the movie theater during previews. it was hard to see in the dark, but we managed with Jonathan leading the way. The seats were the tall kind, like in an airplane, and we sat in them without touching for several minutes. The movie opened with men jumping out of planes, then chasing each other through the air. Teeth were gritted against G forces; parachutes were engaged in the nick of time. At the sight of the first attractive woman with whom Bond would surely make love, I leaned over and kissed Jonathan full on the mouth.

"Jesus Christ," he whispered.

We kissed again. I touched his thigh through his khakis, and imagined the intramural sports he must have played to get the muscles feeling that way. "Jesus Christ," he whispered again, and suddenly I liked that he was in high school, so appreciative, so grateful for the feverish pace of my seduction. I imagined he thought this was the real world talking to him now, and that surely he would be the one to learn new tricks tonight, and not the other way around.

We stopped kissing and tried to return to the movie, but it was impractical. I had missed several scenes and felt disoriented. "Who's that?" I asked Jonathan when a new character appeared on-screen, and he put his tongue in my mouth for an answer. "Should we go?" I whispered in his ear.

"Maybe we'd better," he said.

I was all over him in the car on the way home. I confessed I was a virgin and he laughed and called me a liar. "Liar!" he said again, having a terrible time keeping his hands on the wheel. He wanted at least one down my shirt or under my skirt at all times, and I eventually pulled away, worried for the trips to my college he wouldn't be able to make without a car or his driver's license. I left him alone like that, shirt untucked, pants unbelted and unzipped, erection peeking out from beneath the waistband of his shorts, reaching impressively toward me in the passenger seat.

But Jonathan had abandoned all safety. "Come back!" he yelled frantically. "Get the hell back over here!"

I was all over him.

We went back to his house, where he said we could drink from his parents' liquor cabinet and roll around on their water bed. I might've felt more comfortable at my house, but there was always the chance my mother and Roscoe had ended up there. They slept together even though he was impotent, and my assumption was that he still did things for her. I thought briefly about how my mother had not wanted me to sneak around, but as liberal as she was, that probably just applied to smoking cigarettes.

Jonathan's house was sort of typical, and he seemed embarrassed about this, eyeing me nervously as I scanned the family portraits lining the living room wall. He stood behind a small bar in the corner of the room, cracking ice trays and fumbling the cubes into highballs. "Look at you," I said, marveling over a group shot that included a longer-haired, be-spectacled Jonathan, two sedate-looking parents, and a couple of little boys. I couldn't imagine my mother hanging such things on our walls. Her idea was to rent original art from the library for six months at a time.

"No," Jonathan said. "Don't look at those."

"What else am I supposed to look at?" I asked him. There they all were, lined up in front of me.

"Over there," he said, pointing to the brick mantel. "Look at that."

I followed his finger, which led to a bronze trophy of a young man dressed in a football uniform. "Wow," I said, noting his name engraved at the bottom.

"It's stupid," he admitted.

I shrugged and moved on to another family portrait. The older ones had been taken in front of autumn-scapes and fake bookcases, while the newer ones were backed with the same cloudy blue as a school picture. It seemed the portraits were arranged chronologically, so that the more I moved to the right, the better-looking Jonathan got. He resembled his mother more than his father, though unlike Jonathan, her features did not add up to beauty. It struck me then that it was this that embarrassed him.

"Don't look at those," he told me again. He was opening and closing cupboards, clinking bottles, stirring drinks with his index finger.

I sighed and turned my attention to the various bouquets of dried flowers dotting the room, the homespun knickknacks his mother had either made or picked out. And while it seemed clear that I would never meet this woman—Jonathan would see to that—I still believed her son and I could get married.

"Here," Jonathan said, coming up behind me.

I took the drink from him and we stood in the middle of the room, guzzling gin and tonics.

"Too strong?" he asked me.

"God no."

"That's right," he said, taking my experience into account. "You're nineteen? Twenty?"

I nodded at both. I would turn twenty my first week at college. "I'm a virgin," I reminded him.

He laughed and some of his drink sprayed out his nose. "Stop saying that!" he said.

We finished our drinks and took off all our clothes, leaving them in a heap in the middle of the living room. Jonathan looked me up and down and since I was drunk I said, "I can't help it if I'm beautiful."

"Shit!" he said. "Wait until I compliment you first."

"Why should I?" I said.

He tried to find an answer but couldn't, and this got us both laughing. When he stopped he commanded me: "Go find my room."

I turned and headed for the stairs, and he followed me at a short distance, saying, "Look at that ass! That *ass*!"

"Where the hell is it?" I asked when I got to the second floor.

"Left," he told me. "Now turn around and walk backwards." I did and he said, "Look at those tits!"

I got dizzy then and fell into a wall, and Jonathan ran to catch me, easing me onto the carpet, which was where I wanted to be. A plaque proclaiming HOME IS WHERE THE HEART IS fell on the floor beside me, and Jonathan snatched it up and said, "Don't look at that."

"Where's your bedroom?" I asked him.

"Right here," he said, tossing the plaque in a linen closet. I had fallen down in front of his doorway.

I nodded and started to get up, but he said, "No, no, you'll hurt yourself." Instead he gripped both my ankles, swiveled me, and dragged me into his room on my back.

Now we were really laughing, and I worried slightly that this was no kind of first memory for me. We should stop kidding around, I thought, and take this thing more seriously. "Jonathan," I said, hiking myself up on my elbows. He had his back to me and was fishing around for something in his dresser drawer. The walls were painted some dark color, and pennants hung above his bed. A pompom dangled from one of his bedposts, though it did not occur to me to attach it to a cheerleader. "Jonathan," I said again.

He turned around and let loose an accordion of condoms, like a proud father with a wallet full of pictures. "I want to do it in every room!" he announced.

"Pick one room!" I demanded. "I'm a virgin."

He covered his ears and sang, "La la la la la la la I can't hear you!"

"One room!" I told him, when he could hear again.

He ignored me and slipped a condom on. I made a move for his bed but he said, "Stay down, stay down," lowering himself onto me.

"Ow," I said, though nothing had happened yet. I was preparing myself.

"Are you ready?" he asked me, then he kissed me between my legs for a few minutes. "You're ready, you're ready," he whispered when he came back up.

"Ow," I said again.

"Could you stop saying that?" he asked, pushing himself into me, trying to find the right spot.

"Go easy," I said.

"Stop laughing," he told me.

"Did it pop yet? Did you pop it?"

"You can't say things like that," he warned me. "You have to say something sexy, like my dick is big and hard."

I told him his dick was big and hard and it made him laugh. "Okay, don't say that," he said. He flopped onto the carpet beside me and gave up trying to make love for a minute.

"I told you," I said.

"You're just tense," he countered, getting his second wind. "Okay, stand up." He got up first and held out a hand for me. "You need the water bed. That'll relax you."

"Leopard print?" i said as we walked into his parents' bedroom. I waited for him to tell me not to look at it, but he didn't. It would've been kind of impossible since nearly everything was leopard: the bedspread, the pillows, the rug.

"Lie down in the middle of the bed," he told me, and I did, creating a small wake.

"This bed makes me feel fat," I complained.

"Spread your legs a little," he said, still standing in the doorway.

"No," I told him.

"Squeeze your tits together."

That I did.

"Wait here," he said.

I heard him run down the stairs and come back up again. He was holding a bottle of gin in his hand, and we both drank from it straight.

He got on the bed with me and went down between my legs again. The water bed sloshed with the small movements we made together. It was nice, what Jonathan was doing, and we stopped laughing after a while. I thought he seemed very mature, and full of gifts.

When I was ready again, Jonathan put a new condom on and pushed himself into me, regardless of any resistance. "Oh!" I said.

"Keep going?" he asked me breathlessly. "Can I keep going?"

"Yes," I said. This was the part that really hurt, the keeping-going, but I felt a certain pride in being able to endure it, in knowing that this would only make things easier for me in the future.

Afterward we went in the bathroom together to clean up. "What's that?" I asked Jonathan, pointing to a pastel shift hanging over one of the towel racks.

"That's my mother's nightie," he said, grabbing it and wadding it up. "Don't look at my mother's nightie." He opened the cupboard under the sink and tossed it inside.

"Why not?" I asked him.

He shrugged. "It's a big nightie."

"So?"

He looked down at himself then and saw the blood on his condom. He touched it.

"See!" I told him, delighted at last to have proof.

"Jesus," he said. He wasn't laughing now.

"You *were* my first!" I insisted.

"Oh man," he said, and before our eyes, he lost what was left of his erection.

Jonathan was afraid i would leak blood on his parents' sheets, so he made me sleep on a towel. In the morning, he wadded it up and threw it in the trash, even though it wasn't stained. We got dressed and he drove me back to my house. My mother's car was in the driveway and I asked Jonathan to come in and say hello, but he said he didn't think so. He said he had to go home and get ready for work.

"Me too," I said.

"You work today?" he asked.

I nodded.

"Then I guess I'll see you there."

"I guess so."

We kissed and for a second I was sorry it wasn't last night and we weren't about to do the whole thing over again.

Inside, I was beside myself. My mother wouldn't ask me where I had been the night before—which I saw as a distinct power play on her part—and I was too shy to tell her, so I smoked three cigarettes instead. I got ready for work several hours too early, then called Mina and Evelyn to tell them it was mission accomplished, and that they wouldn't recognize me the next time they saw me.

"You're right," Evelyn said when I came into work that afternoon. "You walk like you're trying to squeeze a cash register between your thighs."

She and Mina laughed at me, and as much as I knew Evelyn was exaggerating, I was glad she didn't tease me by saying I didn't look different at all. They both wanted a blow-by-blow account of what had happened—which I gave them—and we laughed all day at the words *blow-by-blow, cash register,* and *Italian sausage.* In between customers, we picked out lingerie for me to take to college and set it aside in the back room. When Mina went on break, Evelyn told me privately that she was proud of me for going after what I wanted. "Look at you," she said, and she poked me with a satin hanger, which was her way of being affectionate.

When Mina came back from break I asked her if she'd seen Jonathan at the pizza place, but she said no. I was antsy to talk to more people about my experience, so I wandered into the toy store next door, where Doug, who had dumped me earlier that summer, was working. "Hi," I said, sauntering up to his checkout line. The place was pretty quiet. The only time people ever got serious about toys and lingerie was at Christmas.

Doug shoved his hands in the red smock he had to wear, which was probably supposed to get people in the holiday mood, no matter the time of year. It definitely worked on me, but that was only because Doug bore a striking resemblance to an overgrown elf. "Hello, Gilda," he said warily.

"Oh, don't worry," I said. "I'm not after you."

"Do you need a toy?" he asked me, irritated.

"Oh no," I said. "I just came to let you know you lost your chance."

I ran back to Angelina's then and reported this conversation to Evelyn, who thought it was the best thing she'd ever heard—long overdue.

Next I went to the pizza place to see about Jonathan, but he still wasn't there. Renaldo told me he wasn't coming in today. "He's sick."

"No he's not," I said.

Renaldo shrugged.

"I know he's not sick," I said.

Renaldo didn't ask me how I knew.

"I know because I saw him last night *and* this morning."

"Oh yeah?" Renaldo said. He looked over at his son Bert,

who was ladling red sauce onto a round of pizza dough, and they winked at each other. When Renaldo turned back to me, he said, "So how come you no smiling?"

I smiled for him.

"Thatsa good," he said, but it didn't sound the way it used to.

Evelyn dropped me off after work and warned me not to call Jonathan. I told her I wouldn't but it was the first thing I did when I got in the house. "Are you sick?" I asked him, sitting at the little phone desk in one corner of the kitchen so my mother could hear. She was paying her bills at the kitchen table.

"Not really," he said. His voice was cold.

"Well, should I come over?"

My mother closed her checkbook, capped her pen, then walked out of the room. When I heard the front door open I covered the receiver and called after her, "Wait, where are you going?"

"It's helmet night at the stadium," she yelled back. "While supplies last!"

"Wait!" I commanded my mother again, and she did, with the door still open. I quickly asked Jonathan, "You want to go to a baseball game? My mom works for the Chiefs, so it's free."

"No thanks," he said.

"That's okay, Mom!" I yelled, covering the receiver again. "We'll pass!" The door shut and she was gone. "So should I come over?" I said, returning to Jonathan.

"It's up to you," he told me.

"It's not that far," I said. "I'll just walk."

We made love again on his parents' water bed, and this time it didn't hurt as much. I still didn't have an orgasm, but I figured that would come in time. Afterward Jonathan said I should probably go, and that he would drive me home since it was dark. We got dressed and went downstairs, where earlier I had kicked off my sneakers. Suddenly I was tired of pretending nothing was wrong, and I started to cry. "What happened?" I asked him. "Why don't you like me anymore?"

He shrugged. I was sitting on his mother's flowery couch and he was standing in front of me, jingling his car keys. I could tell he thought it was taking me forever to lace up my shoes. "Huh?" I said, prodding him.

"You handled this whole thing all wrong," he said finally.

"Why?"

"Because we're not in love. You don't give it away if you're not in love."

"I love you," I said, trying to rectify things.

"Tie your shoes, will you?"

I bent over and started tying them.

He said, "You're desperate, that's your problem."

"How do you know?" I asked him.

"I have eyes."

This got me started on a new cycle of crying, blurring my vision so that I tied my shoelaces in knots. "I'm vulnerable," I told him. "I'm making myself vulnerable to you because I love you."

"Stop saying that," he said.

"Okay," I said, giving up on my sneakers. "I'll just think it." I stood up and faced him. He told me to hold on for a second, then went into a small bathroom off the foyer and returned with a pink quilted tissue dispenser. "Here," he said, holding the box out to me. "You're ruining your makeup."

"It's already ruined," I complained, taking a tissue anyway.

"No it's not," he said. He took a tissue, too, and worked it carefully around my eyes, which only made me cry harder. I knew this was it, that the next time I saw him he would be colder than ever and there would be nothing I could do about it.

"See," I said, as he continued to dot my face gingerly. "You still like me."

"I never said I didn't like you," he said.

At work a few days later i came clean with Evelyn. About everything. "I told you not to call him," she scolded me, but she laid off when I started crying. She did make me promise not to beg Jonathan as I had done with Doug, and I meant it when I said I wouldn't. For a second she looked as if she were going to cry, too. I thought about hugging her, but I was saving that for the day I left. Finally she looked up at the ceiling and asked God, "Where did I go wrong?" We both laughed at the idea that she could be my mother, and before things got too sentimental, she excused herself to get her heel fixed.

I went in the back room and gathered up the lingerie the

three of us had picked out for me. As I put it all back on the racks, Mina said, "No! Not that one!" about a camisole she was particularly fond of. I thought about how much I liked her and Evelyn then, and how much I would miss them once I was gone.

Evelyn had still not returned when I was finished with the lingerie, so I fished Jonathan's baseball out of my purse and asked Mina if she would give it to him after I left. We were standing behind the cash register like we always did, ignoring all the customers.

"No problem," Mina said, and I appreciated the way she quickly put the ball into her own purse.

"Do you think I'm doing the wrong thing?" I asked her a few minutes later.

She laughed and shook back her long brown hair, with all its strange layers and broken ends. "Of course not," she said. "It has his name on it."

The Brutal Language of Love

Penny stood on a stepladder outside the movie theater where she worked, changing posters in the glass cases. It was between rushes on a Monday afternoon, and Fritz was ignoring her from inside the ticket booth, hunched over an old sociology textbook. A thin blond man approached the ticket window and asked Fritz a question. Fritz pointed to Penny, then returned to his book. The man nodded and began walking her way. For a second she wondered if she had a secret admirer, or had won the Publishers Clearing House. But he was only a film student from the local university, wanting to make a documentary about projectionists.

Penny was slightly disappointed, but agreed to appear in

the man's movie. He said his name was Leonard and told Penny he just wanted to ask her a few questions and film her doing her job in the projection booth. "A piece of cake," he said. They shook hands and set a date. Penny checked to see if Fritz had witnessed any of this, but he was still reading.

Fritz was a college dropout who had worked his way up from concessionaire to head of floorstaff. Penny, who had barely managed to graduate and was subsequently rejected from business school, had worked her way up to projectionist. They had met and fallen in love at the theater, where they immediately began cultivating a torturous history filled with breakups and crying. Most of this took place between rushes, in the privacy of the projection booth. They always got back together, though, Fritz missing the sex and Penny the love. She supposed if she had friends they would tell her this wasn't really love, but she was upstairs in the dark most of the time, developing only her relationship with Fritz.

When Penny told Fritz about Leonard's documentary, he didn't bat an eyelid. For it was generally Fritz doing the breaking up and Penny the crying—followed by the pining—thereby rendering him incapable of jealousy. Oh well, Penny thought, retreating to the booth so she could unbutton her white work shirt and feel the lump in her right breast: she was facing grave illness now and that was all that mattered. Fritz was genuinely concerned for her; she didn't need jealousy to keep him.

Meanwhile, she had no health insurance. She worked as many as fifty hours a week sometimes, but her job description was officially part-time, and she was nonunion. However, for such a serious medical condition, she felt her father, a wealthy immigrant who held her in low esteem, might be willing to cover expenses. She saw this as something over which they might come together, a way to help him forget that she had not gotten into graduate school.

Penny called her father collect from her office in the projection booth, where everything was coated in a thin layer of mechanical grease. It was more embarrassing to say the word *breast* to him than to ask for money, though she managed both. His answer was no. Penny became hysterical and her father complained he could understand little of what she said when she was crying. As soon as she quieted down he said no again, this time with more sympathy in his voice. Penny touched the lump in her breast to make sure she wasn't imagining things. "But why?" she asked him.

"Try to understand," her father said. "You're twenty-five years of age. I can't keep giving you money."

"I know," she said.

"You need a job which provides insurance."

"Uh-huh," she said.

"Somehow you must move into the business world, which is burgeoning. A secretarial position in which you could rise through the ranks would be ideal."

"I can't type."

"You could pursue a typing course. I would be willing to pay for that."

"Could I take the money for the typing course and put it towards my biopsy?"

"The money is applicable only to typing."

Penny started to cry again. "Why?"

"I told you, Penelope. I can't understand you when you weep."

She calmed herself down. "I feel depressed."

He said, "I already paid for therapy."

"I know."

"Sometimes we just have to pull ourselves up and forget how we feel."

"I know I would feel less depressed if you would help me with my biopsy," Penny said, trying out the straightforward language the therapist had taught her.

"In fact you wouldn't," her father said. "And if you stop to think about it, a typing course does help with your biopsy because it will lead you to a job offering health benefits."

"But I can't wait that long. The surgeon says I need a biopsy now."

"Have you gotten a second opinion?"

"I can't afford one."

"I would be willing to pay for that."

Penny was losing control of herself again. "I can't leave my job," she cried. "I love Fritz."

"Once again," her father said, irritated, "I can no longer comprehend you."

"Fritz!" she said loudly. "I like working with him."

"But it doesn't matter where you work! If Fritz loves you now, he can only love you more once you make self-improvements."

"It does matter," she insisted.

"Fritz," her father mumbled. "This is an unsuitable character. Which traits does he possess after which you might model yourself?"

"He's worried about me," Penny said.

"I'm worried about you," her father countered.

This made her feel better for a moment—younger—so she said, "Please help me this one last time, Daddy."

She hadn't called him that for many years and it silenced him momentarily. "Well," her father said at last, "I have decided I will help you. Okay. What you will do is the following."

He explained that she should contact every free clinic and welfare office in the city, looking for financial assistance. Even if the answer was no, she should be sure to obtain documentation of at least having tried, for he could not write any checks without such proof of her efforts. "So you see, you can depend upon me this one last time," he concluded.

"Thank you," Penny said.

"But really, Penelope, you're much too old for this."

"Yes," she said, drying her face.

"A job in the business world would require a neat haircut and a navy blue business suit, both of which I would be willing to subsidize," he added.

"I'll think about it after the biopsy," she said, "if I don't have cancer."

"If you do have it you'll definitely need health insurance," he noted.

"I agree," she said.

"I love you," he said.

"I love you, too."

"I will purchase a bus ticket for you to come and see me as soon as you specify a date."

"Okay," she said, and they hung up.

He lived only a couple of hours away, and liked to tell her when she visited that she should think of his home as a spa, a place where she could just relax and forget all her troubles. If she had packed a modest ensemble, he might schedule an evening out with friends from work or his church. These were invariably kind people who had a clear affinity for Penny's father, and so she studied them closely, anxious to learn how she—his own daughter—had managed to misplace her affections.

Fritz came to see her between the five and seven o'clock rushes, and listened as Penny described the conversation with her father. She cried again when she was finished, and Fritz held her close, his black polyester work vest scratchy against her face. "Don't worry about money anymore," he said, moving his hand lightly across her shoulder blades, then down over her bottom. He brought it back up again, around front, and began unbuttoning her work shirt. "I'll check your lump," he murmured, squeezing her breast in gentle, concentric circles. His chest was broad from lifting fifty-pound bags of unpopped corn, his erection persistent against her stomach.

The day of the interview was at hand. Leonard arrived with a scraggly classmate, Max, who would run the video camera. They set up their equipment in Penny's office, while she made her way down the length of the projection booth—really the entire second floor of the theater—threading all the two o'clock shows. It was an old fourplex that screened art movies, and sometimes the governor, who was cultured, showed up on weekends.

For the interview they seated Penny on a stool at her work table, where she built all the films that came into the theater. They shone lamps on her and clipped a microphone to her favorite orange T-shirt. Leonard turned her face gently to show her how to catch the light, and she felt conscious of any makeup that might have rubbed off on his hands, though he didn't seem pressed to wash them later.

"Can I get you to say something so I can check my levels?" Max said, sitting on the floor behind his camera tripod and a sound mixer.

Penny read from a poster on the wall above him: "*Stanno Tutti Bene.*"

"That's an Italian film, right?" he asked.

Penny nodded. "Yes."

"Any good?"

"I didn't see it," she said.

He turned a few knobs and said, "Ever get tired of reading subtitles?"

"Not really," she said. Then she added, "It's a lot better than dubbing."

"Perfect," Max said, turning one last knob, and Penny understood he didn't care whether she was tired of subtitles or not.

Leonard took a standing position beside the tripod and they began. He had promised to ask Penny questions, but instead just said, "Tell me what it's like to be a projectionist," and, "Talk about whatever you want." Penny felt disappointed by his lack of guidance but obliged him by rambling— admitting, for instance, that she never watched movies from the booth because the sound was terrible. She went on to describe the perks of her job—naps and free movies—as well as the dangers, such as changing the volatile projector bulbs. For this, regulations specified she wear a welding mask and leather gloves, and at Leonard's request, Penny modeled these items before the camera.

When at last she had run out of work-related conversation, Penny told Leonard about her breast. She had a choice between a biopsy for eight hundred dollars or a lumpectomy for two thousand, both of which were considered minor procedures. Her surgeon was pushing the lumpectomy, but that was him, he had told her—he liked to cut things out. He was a vegetarian who worked in a wood-frame house, and Penny appreciated the way he gazed at the ceiling while examining her. If she qualified for assistance she would undoubtedly have to see someone else, which concerned her, since she didn't want anyone looking her in the eye over this.

Still, she had gone to the welfare office with her two most recent check stubs, dressed purposely in clothes that were too small for her and in need of repair. If she didn't look poor enough, she worried, the caseworkers might suspect her of having a rich parent and cart her away for fraud. In the crowded waiting room, she watched a little girl wearing sandals and only one sock braid her father's ponytail. Penny's own father's hair was coarse and made little ripping sounds when he ran a comb through it.

Later, in a fluorescent cubicle, a kind man with a foggy right eye regretted to inform Penny that she earned too much to qualify for benefits. He said she could cut her hours and come back again with two new pay stubs, but she explained this wouldn't be possible since she might have cancer, and time was of the essence. The man nodded gravely, and instead of rushing her out, observed a moment of silence for her difficulties. This had moved Penny deeply at the time, and again now, as she recounted the meeting for Leonard. She took a second to gather herself before concluding, "He would've helped me if he could."

"Did you, um, look elsewhere?" Leonard asked, posing his first real question of the day.

A few places, she told him. But then she got depressed and didn't follow through. In the end she chose the biopsy because it was cheaper, and called the hospital billing department to set up a long-term payment plan.

The graduate students looked at her. After a moment, Leonard cleared his throat and asked, "Would you prefer the lumpectomy?"

Penny started to cry. "Yes," she said. "I would. I want it out. Even if it's benign I want it out."

She had not known this about herself, and having just revealed it to strangers made her cry all the more. Max quickly readjusted his sound levels and gave Leonard a firm thumbs-up. Penny felt very lonely and unhappy sitting there while the two of them taped her, yet she couldn't bring herself to ask them to stop. Leonard looked too thrilled, like he was going to get an A on his project with all this crying, and for some reason Penny wanted him to get an A.

Later, she followed the students downstairs and into the lobby, with its teal rug and red velvet cordons. "This is Max and Leonard," she called to Fritz, who stood beside the popcorn machine looking smart in his black bow tie.

"Good interview?" he asked, and they all three nodded.

In the parking lot, Penny watched as they loaded the equipment into the trunk of Leonard's hatchback. Max shook her hand and said, "I know you'll be fine," which made Penny think he had been listening after all. He waited in the passenger seat while Leonard hesitated, playing with his keys. "I just want you to know," Leonard said finally. "Well, I'll drop the tape off when it's done."

"Okay," she said. He was wearing shorts and sandals and she could tell he had not bathed before coming to see her. She now knew two of the most intimate things she could know about him: he had somewhat jumbled-looking toes and his personal odor was not unpleasant. It had taken months for Fritz to reveal his feet to Penny, deformed as they were from ill-fitting childhood shoes, and he always, always wore deodorant.

Fritz took Penny to the biopsy. He said silly things in the waiting room about *Reader's Digest* and plastic foliage to try to make her laugh, but it didn't work. Penny was terrified. She would be awake for the procedure, and was not at all comforted by the idea of a shot of Novocain to her breast. She would be given Valium to protect her from the pain of the shot, but understood that tranquilizers only really worked when you knew nothing was coming.

The nurse called her name and Fritz stood up, too. For a moment Penny thought he was going to insist on accompanying her, but then he sat back down again, as adults were expected to do. He looked more distraught than she had ever seen him—jerky and wild-eyed—and she greedily soaked up his concern before leaving the room.

The procedure involved lying prostrate on a table with holes cut into it, so that Penny's face and right breast hung beneath her. Her breast was then immobilized in a sort of vise grip, making it thankfully difficult to discern the pain of the first shot—and all those that followed—from the general ache in her chest. The nurses worked quickly, sympathizing over the discomfort she must be feeling, but aches were of no consequence to Penny. They came on so slowly that the only time you ever really noticed them was if and when they went away.

When her breast was numb, a specialist breezed in, introduced himself, and set to work inserting a sharp little spatula into her lump. He did this several times, and though Penny could not see his face, she did make out the squiggly pieces of flesh he withdrew from beneath the table. This was it, the stuff she was made of, and it struck her that there might indeed be something wrong with it.

Afterward she was left with a small puncture wound. The

nurse said her surgeon would call as soon as the results were in, and escorted Penny out into the waiting area. "I was so worried about you," Fritz said, standing up to meet her. She cried on the way home when he presented her with a crisp one-hundred-dollar bill, saying that, after all, it was his breast, too.

At her garage apartment, he got her settled in bed and took off her shirt and bra to assess the damage. "You can't take off the bandage yet," she warned him, drowsy from the Valium. "It looks like a snake bite."

He nodded and backed away. She must have fallen asleep then because when she awoke her shirt was back on and Fritz was gone. Later, before bed, she would discover that her dressing had been expertly changed, an even better job than the nurses had done.

The phone woke Penny the next morning. She sat up and looked around, momentarily unsure of where she was in the continuum of her life until the ache in her chest reminded her that at least the biopsy was over. A large roach skittered behind one of the movie posters on her wall, and Penny felt a great relief when it never reemerged. She reached for the receiver on the bedside stand and said, "Hello."

"Penny? It's Leonard."

"Leonard." She propped her pillow up behind her head. For a second she couldn't place the name.

"From the interview?"

"Oh right," she said. "I just had my biopsy."

"I know. I'm calling to see if you're okay."

She felt her mind clearing then. "How do you know?"

"You told me the date. Remember?"

"No."

"Oh," he said. "Well, I was wondering if I could come over and film you."

"Why?"

"For closure," he said. "So my audience will know you're all right."

"I don't want to be filmed now."

"Hmm," he said.

"I don't even know if I'm all right."

"When will you know?"

"Soon, I guess."

"Can I film you then?"

"What does this have to do with projectionists?" Penny asked.

"Well," Leonard said, "I changed my topic. My new topic is breast cancer."

"Oh," she said.

"I was inspired by your interview."

"Uh-huh."

"Could I come over now without the camera?"

"I have a boyfriend, Leonard."

"Really?" he said. "Who?"

"That guy I introduced you to at the theater. Who makes popcorn. Remember him?"

"Vaguely."

"Fritz. That's my boyfriend."

"Is he over there now?"

"No."

"Hmm," Leonard said again.

"I mean, were you wanting to come over for a date?"

"I hadn't really thought about it," he said.

"Because I guess you could come over as a friend. If you want."

He considered this briefly. "Okay then. How about that?"

"Sure," Penny said, and she gave him her address. After they hung up she considered cleaning her apartment, but couldn't get up the energy. Maybe Leonard would tidy it for her, she thought. Maybe Leonard would bring his camera anyway, and force her to show him her breast. At this Penny suddenly burst into tears, unsure of how she would stop him.

But Leonard brought only flowers—blue ones, which he cut down and arranged in an old mayonnaise jar, then placed at Penny's bedside. Next, as if he had read her mind, he began straightening magazines and washing dirty dishes. At her request, he tapped all the movie posters on the wall, capturing the roaches that came out from behind them in an old yogurt tub. "Don't kill them," Penny reminded him, and she watched out her window as he set them free in the front yard. He was polite but firm with her upon his return: "If you don't make a home for roaches, Penny, they won't make a home with you."

After vacuuming her shag carpet and scrubbing her bath-room sink, Leonard sat down on the floor beside Penny's bed and read to her from her favorite women's magazines. She re-quested articles about how to increase one's bust size and the allure of animal-print underwear, as well as a love quiz, which Leonard scored in pencil. He read the questions softly, as if they were some kind of lullaby, and Penny dozed off, under-standing that while he might stare at her as she slept, he would never touch her.

She awoke several hours later to find that instead of leav-ing, Leonard too had fallen asleep, a copy of *Cosmo* tucked beneath his head. He was a tall man and Penny suspected if she asked any of the female ushers at the theater, they would describe him as cute, with his long blond eyelashes and square-cut jaw.

But Penny resisted him. He was hers for the taking, and this was the problem. Love was never easy, she knew. And if it was, it wasn't love—friendship maybe, but not love. What she felt for Leonard was something limp and slack. It had no charge, no current running through it to hurt her if she wasn't careful. The reality was, you only knew you were loved if you were left and returned to, if you were ignored and then craved. Occasionally you would be seen for slightly less than the sum of your parts, and that was love, too. Love an-nounced itself with a sting, not a pat. If love was love, it was urgent and ripe and carried with it the faint odor of humilia-tion, so that there was always something to be made up for later, some apology in the works. Love was never clean, never quiet, never polite. Love rarely did what you asked it to, let alone what you dreamed it might do, and it most certainly did not know that your favorite color was blue.

Penny's surgeon called to say her lump was benign. She called her father to tell him the news but there was no answer. She left messages on his machine but he never called back. "Maybe he's on vacation," Fritz told her.

"Maybe," Penny said. But he usually called when he went out of town, giving her his itinerary and joking about how if his plane went down, she would at last have all the money she desired.

"Well, then maybe he's just mad," Fritz concluded.

"About what?" she said.

He shrugged. It was a Thursday evening and they were trudging out to the edge of the parking lot to change the marquee for the coming week. Penny lugged an old duffel bag filled with big black letters, while Fritz carried the ladder. "I don't know," he said. "Not following through with the public assistance?"

"But he didn't have to pay anything," Penny said. "Why should he care?"

Fritz shrugged. "He made you an offer and you never got back to him. Maybe he thought he was doing you some big favor."

Penny stopped walking and looked at him blankly.

"I'm just trying to think like he does!" Fritz protested, slowing once he realized she was no longer beside him. "Hurry up, will you? This thing's heavy."

"Coming," she said, catching up.

"You get so mad," he grumbled.

They stopped at the base of the marquee. Fritz propped his ladder against the steel post so that it nearly touched a second, attached ladder farther up—the one that would take them to the platform at the top. Penny dropped the duffel bag on the asphalt, loving the rattle of the nearly indestructible plastic letters, and tied a rope around its handles so they could pull it up later. A section of her unruly hair blew wildly in front of her face and Fritz reached over and tucked it behind her ear. Almost instantly it flew back out again, and he pushed it back again, holding it there, stepping in to kiss her bare cheek. "Don't come up here today," he told her. "It's too windy."

She followed him anyway, captivated by the spell of his concern.

Unlike Penny's father, Leonard had been calling her incessantly. She could only conclude there was something wrong with him that he should worry so unduly over someone he hardly knew. When she finally gave him her test results he insisted they go out and celebrate, but she declined. "Fritz doesn't want me to see you anymore," she said, trying to sound convincing. "He thinks you're after me."

When she later suggested to Fritz that Leonard might in fact be after her, he agreed this was entirely possible, but took no preventive measures.

At work one afternoon she found an old pornographic reel from the seventies and ran it for Fritz after closing. Her snake bite had finally healed, and she was anxious to present her smooth-skinned self to him—to celebrate with the man who had detected her lump in the first place, though he had not specifically been looking for it. Fritz found the movie mostly humorous—the hairdos, pant legs, et cetera—but stopped laughing when Penny got up out of her seat and attempted to mimic the actresses. Afterward he told her he had an even better idea, and that she should wait in the auditorium while he went upstairs to thread another movie, a skill Penny had taught him. When he returned, Fritz instructed her, she should pretend he was a stranger, remain seated, and it would be clear what he wanted her to do.

They began spending several hours a week like this, unbuttoning themselves in the dark auditoriums and pretending they'd never met. To lend authenticity to their nights, they stopped speaking to each other during the day. The rest of the theater staff thought they had broken up again, though they seemed confused by Penny's lack of sorrow, her dry, unpuffy eyes.

Back in her apartment, Penny dreamt of Leonard, who had begun coming to the theater with a stout blond woman. He had given up on Penny—barely even turned around anymore to watch her start the movies—which at last gave him some kind of appeal. In Penny's dreams, Leonard would drive her to Fritz's apartment, wait for her to have sex with Fritz, then drive her home, smiling as if this were all in the course of a day. "Same time tomorrow night?" he'd ask, and she'd nod, waving as he pulled away. In her waking hours, she began plotting to depose his new girlfriend, though she would never actually do it. If only things could stay exactly this way, Penny thought: Fritz, the stranger who liked to screw her, and Leonard, whose presence was beginning to sting.

it was a Wednesday night and Penny was attaching new trailers to the movies, while downstairs, Fritz stored the nacho cheese sauce and rinsed grease from the hot dog rotisserie. Though they still weren't speaking, he had found a way to communicate with her through the use of marquee numbers. Earlier that evening, for example, she had arrived at work to find a plastic 2 hanging from her office door. This meant she should report to that particular auditorium after the last shows let out. The friends she didn't have would surely have told her to end all this now, yet night after night she sat alone in the dark, awaiting further instructions from Fritz. For it was her grave concern that if they stopped pretending they were strangers, they would not necessarily resume speaking.

As each of the movies ended that night, Penny shut down the projectors, then covered them with sheets of protective plastic. In her private bathroom, she inserted her diaphragm, though she didn't always need it. On her way downstairs she passed Fritz coming up. While they didn't acknowledge each other, Penny noted the videotape in his hand. The booth was also equipped with video projectors, and sometimes, for a change, Fritz brought movies from home. His favorites were old black-and-white productions from the Eastern bloc in which sullen girls with dyed blond hair and runny eyeliner search for romance in postwar Europe. Often Penny wondered if Fritz didn't wish he had lived back then, meeting the raggedy girls of his dreams and whispering to them in a brutal language of love.

In Auditorium 2, Penny picked the aisle seat of a middle row, which would afford them extra room for maneuvering. As she waited for Fritz, her phantom pains began: sharp pricks in the area of her biopsy. The surgeon said it was nothing serious, and to remember that she had, after all, undergone an invasive procedure; such wounds could take up to three months to heal. Meanwhile, Penny thought of the pains as nagging, bratty children who wanted more attention than they deserved, and she reveled in her ability to ignore them.

Slowly the lights dimmed. Penny had an urge to look back at Fritz and wave, but knew he wouldn't like that, so she stayed put. She waited now for an image of a smoking factory; a barren winter landscape; a set of dirty, feminine fingertips lighting an unfiltered cigarette before exhaling a combination of smoke and frost from between chapped lips. Instead, she saw her father.

He was a bulky, gray-haired man getting out of a late-model Saab. He carried with him a bag of groceries and a briefcase as he approached the front door of a large, colonial-looking home. Penny heard Leonard's voice next, though she couldn't actually see him: "Excuse me, sir, but is it true you won't pay for your daughter's biopsy? Sir?" Her father turned around then, looking irritated without having to change his natural expression. "Sir," Leonard persisted, "is it true your daughter may have cancer and you don't even care?" A boom microphone dipped briefly in front of her father's face, and he slapped it away. It fell to the ground and Leonard's friend Max appeared quickly, retrieving it. "I'm calling the police and I have a handgun," Penny's father warned, turning his back on the camera and letting himself into the house.

Now, in the theater, Penny could hear the jingle of Fritz's belt buckle behind her. She would not be able to see the screen when he took his position in front of her, so she quickly got up and moved forward, picking a new seat at the center of the second row.

Meanwhile, a shot of a pool party in her father's back-yard was materializing. Many adults, some of whom Penny recognized, lounged around in their bathing suits, while her father stood at a gas grill passing out hamburgers to their kids. The camera zoomed in on the pool, the grill, patio furniture, rubber rafts, snorkel equipment, and a weimaraner her father had recently acquired. Each of these shots was accompanied by Leonard's somber voice quoting dollar values: the grill was a thousand, the snorkel equipment a hundred, the puppy—which Leonard guessed to be a purebred—four-fifty. A clump of foliage in the bottom right corner of the frame indicated to Penny that Leonard had shot this footage secretly, in the thick hedge lining her father's property. At one point a young boy who was angry with his mother came to pout directly in front of the camera, prompting Leonard to value his hamburger at fifty cents.

Interspersed with all this was Penny discussing her lump, Penny crying, Penny glowing from the cast of warm lights upon her face. It was disorienting to her now that this story should make any sense, and she immediately stood up, scanning the rows behind her for Fritz. "Where did you get this?" she called out. It was the first time she had spoken to him in weeks, and for a second she thought it could not possibly have been her. "Hello!" she yelled, more to test her vocal equipment than anything else. "Fritz!"

She saw him then, scrunched down in the seat she had vacated earlier, his clip tie undone and dangling from one side of his collar. The credits began to roll on Leonard's video as Penny filed out of her row and started up the aisle. "Where did you get this?" she repeated, for Fritz had still not answered. She stopped beside his chair and looked down at him.

"That guy Leonard dropped it off," he said finally. "He came in with some girl and dropped it off."

"He didn't ask to see me?"

Fritz shrugged. "I said I would take it."

"So he did ask to see me?"

Fritz stood up then. He buckled his belt and sighed. "He said either way was fine: for me to give it to you, or for him to give it to you." The documentary was over now as they stood there, arguing in the dark. "Look," Fritz said, "let's just forget it."

"I need a ride," Penny told him.

"Of course I'll give you a ride," he said.

In Fritz's car she felt she understood everything: why it

was her father had never returned her phone calls, how he must have thought she was the mastermind behind Leonard's documentary. She had been wrong in thinking Leonard hardly knew her, but now that he knew too much, her instinct was to distract him. Maybe she would point out that he had strayed somewhat from his topic of breast cancer, or warn him of her father's litigious nature. Beyond that, Penny had a general interest in anything her father might have said off-camera, and possibly she wanted to thank Leonard, though this was only an idea she was toying with, and who even knew where he lived.

They were riding south on a strip lined with pawn-shops and outdated neon signs advertising burger joints. They passed gun-and-knife stores with barred windows, an abandoned plaza, a lone doughnut shop, outside of which a baker was taking his break. This was the stuff of her affair with Fritz, Penny suddenly realized, and she held her breath until they had driven by, touched a button on her work shirt as she did when passing a hearse. "We need a phone book," she announced when she was breathing again.

Fritz didn't answer.

"What's Leonard's last name?" she demanded. It had appeared at the end of his documentary.

Still no response.

"Fritz!" Penny insisted.

"Lobel," he said.

"That's right," she said. It was all coming back to her.

"You're going to be with him now?" Fritz asked.

"Pull in here," she said, pointing to a 7-Eleven.

He parked under a well-lit self-service island and left the motor running. Inside the store, a middle-aged man in a green smock lent Penny his phone book and watched as she flipped through the residential listings. "You okay there, sugar?" he asked. He peeked out the window at Fritz.

"I'm okay," she said, passing the directory back to him. "Could I use your phone?"

The man laughed. "Not if you're okay. If you're okay you can use the pay phone outside."

But it was no use. Information had no listing for Leonard Lobel. He must have roommates, Penny thought. People who saw him all the time, shared his meals, trusted him enough to list his phone bill in their name.

"Any luck?" Fritz asked when she got back to the car.

She shook her head and said, "Just drive."

He nodded and began roaming the streets surrounding the campus, slowing down in front of houses whose lights were still on, coasting by thinning parties that had spilled out onto the sidewalk. They searched for the stout blond woman and Max, too—anyone who would lead them to Leonard. "It's no use," Penny moaned a couple of hours later. "They're regular people and they're asleep right now."

Fritz ignored her and continued driving, keeping his eyes peeled. Eventually the slow and steady ride of the car sent Penny to sleep. There she dreamed combinations of numbers that might connect her to Leonard, followed by a word jazz of street names she feared did not really exist: Hatchback, Mayonnaise, Eyelash.

When she awoke the car was stopped, parked in front of a large, windowless university building. Fritz was still awake, humming an old polka under his breath.

"What's this?" Penny asked, looking up at the cement structure.

"The Communications Building," he told her.

She nodded.

"Do you know why it doesn't have any windows?" he asked.

She reseated herself so that she faced him more, taking some of the pressure off her rear, which was sore. "Why?" she said.

"Because it's filled with studios. When you shoot in a studio, you need complete control of the lights."

"Oh right," Penny said.

"I took a film class once," he said.

At eight o'clock the students began arriving. They looked different from her and Fritz, Penny thought, with their colorful clothing, and the halos of frizz above their slept-on heads. They carried backpacks, shoulder bags, and half-eaten fruit. When they spoke, it was in earnest over newly adopted theories, or the political ideologies that had begun to rule their lives. When they walked alone, their lips moved.

At a little after eleven Leonard finally appeared, wearing shorts and sandals as he had the day of the interview. He carried a battered leather satchel on his shoulder and was no longer with the blond woman.

"It's exciting," Fritz said suddenly, turning to Penny, and she was compelled to let him touch her hair before getting out of the car.

Still life with Plaster

Grandpa put bricks beneath either end of a wooden plank, creating a sort of table so that Tensie, the dog, would not have to bend down while he ate. Tensie ate out back on the cement porch, or else in the kitchen, beside the stove. He wasn't allowed in the living room with the rest of the family and he wasn't allowed upstairs. On cold nights, when he stayed home, he lay on the kitchen side of the doorway leading into the living room, his two front paws extended just across the threshold. "Tensie!" Grandpa yelled, sensitive to any peripheral infraction, and the dog quickly retreated. I think Tensie wanted not to come in but, rather, to be noticed by Grandpa. Had he just been lying there, following all the rules, his chances might not have been so good.

Grandma hated the dog, and resented the fact that Tensie liked her despite this. "Animals stick to me like glue," she complained when Tensie fell asleep at her feet, his pointy, brown-spotted nose resting lightly on her magnificent bunions. "I have no idea why."

"Because you ignore them," my mother told her. "The same reason *I* like you."

"Don't you talk therapy to me," Grandma warned, and then they got into it, about how Grandma equated going to therapy with climbing to the top of a tall building and throwing twenty-dollar bills off of it, while Mom felt she was finally learning to love herself.

"Love yourself?" Grandma said. "Love yourself? I never saw anyone love herself more! If I had loved myself half as much as you do, you and Dalton would have grown up with Grammy Sue!" Grammy Sue was Grandma's mother, who had been known for hating children.

"I can't go to graduate school and take care of two kids!" Mom yelled.

"So give them to their father!" Grandma yelled back. Then Mom started crying, since the last time we stayed with our father he beat us up pretty good. "Oh never mind," Grandma said, and she gave Mom a tissue. Though I often eavesdropped on these conversations, they never once hurt my feelings. I knew Grandma loved me way more than Mom and almost as much as Dalton, and that her hurtful comments were only designed to get Mom out of the house faster. I admired Grandma for this, as I wanted Mom to leave, too. Until she was gone, I always worried that she would try to take us home with her.

Mom came to see me and my little brother, Cliff, on weekends. She lived in the city, half an hour away, where she was studying to be a special-education teacher. She wanted to help blind, deaf, and retarded kids who needed her, she said. I thought of telling her I needed her, too, but it wasn't true. We had a better family with Grandma and Grandpa. There were a lot of rules you had to follow, and I thought this was an interesting way to live. I didn't like to eat what I wanted or pick my own bedtime, which were things we did with Mom. Instead, I preferred to do the same things, the same way, over and over again. I knew that one day we would return to Mom and her looser way of life, though naturally I hoped she would forget all about us.

My grandparents lived on a couple of acres in the country. When you stepped outside the back door and onto the cement porch, your eye followed a hill down to a wooden fence, where Grandma had pitched her clothesline. It was the square metal kind, hung with plastic cording that made it look like one of the God's-eyes we assembled in art class. Grandma hung clothes out to dry even in winter, which seemed like it wouldn't work, but it did. If you put them on too soon after she brought them in, you would shake all day from the chill.

No matter the season, you could always smell the septic tank. It was located in a marshy area off to the side of the house that you were advised not to step in while you were playing outdoors. Everyone complained about the odor, including me, but secretly I loved it. As obvious as the signs were, it simply did not occur to me that this was shit.

On gym days, i tried to wear dresses to school so that I could leave my tights on when I changed into my shorts. This prevented the other girls from seeing my yellow underpants, which offended them and prompted them to sing songs about how I had urinated on myself. I had other problems. Earlier that year, I had skipped from the second grade, where I had been very popular, to the third, where I was thought to be a rat fink. When I asked my new classmates what this meant, they said, "Well, a rat is someone who tattletales and so is a fink."

"That's redundant," I told them, which would have impressed the second graders I used to know, but had a poor effect on the third.

"What the hell does that mean, turkey?" they said, and then they pushed me in the sandbox. Some of the kids from second grade who were on the playground at the time saw this and looked away, not wanting to believe what had become of me.

Eventually I became friends with a small group of boys who tortured the class gerbil, Henri, and later, me. To win their favor, I brought in an old Fisher-Price snowmobile with little round holes in which to set the accompanying figurines. "You still play with this crap?" a boy named Corbin asked me.

"God no," I told him. "My brother does and I kick his ass

for it!" We stuffed the gerbil in the snowmobile and pushed him around the table until he hopped out and started running. He fell off the edge of the table and the whole class crowded around as he landed on the floor and continued walking, dragging a limp, broken leg behind him. "Henri is injured!" Mrs. Walpin cried. "Who has injured Henri?"

The boys who were my friends pointed to me and—not wanting to be a rat fink—I bravely stepped forward. Mrs. Walpin called Grandma then, who came to collect me and Henri and take us to Tensie's vet. He suggested we put Henri to sleep, which sounded good until Grandma informed me he wouldn't be waking up, at which point I began to cry like a baby. "Oh for godssakes," Grandma said, handing me a tissue from her embroidered purse. "What else have you got?" she asked the vet.

"Well," he said, picking Henri up by his tail and placing him in the palm of his hand, "here's an idea." In the end, Grandma paid forty dollars to have Henri's little leg shaved and wrapped in white surgical tape, which he chewed through by the time we got back to school. All the kids gathered around to watch as he attempted to use the exercise wheel in his Habitrail, then tumbled off it onto a pile of fetid wood chips. Mrs. Walpin set her jaw and asked if I had learned my lesson. I said I had. "Well," she said, "what is it?"

"Hold up," Grandma said. "Patty wasn't the only one involved here."

"Is that so?" Mrs. Walpin asked Grandma. She was snotty, like a bank teller or a saleslady in a department store.

"Tell her, Patty," Grandma said, and I had to, or else Grandma said I would owe her forty dollars, which I knew I wouldn't have for several years.

"Corbin, Jared, and Arthur," I told Mrs. Walpin.

Mrs. Walpin paused, then said, "Would the boys Patty Potocki just named please stand up?"

They stood.

"Is Patty Potocki telling the truth?" she asked them. Two nodded and one shook his head but, when he saw the other boys, changed his no to a yes.

"All right then," Mrs. Walpin sighed, "off to the principal's office."

As they shuffled out, someone hissed, "Rat fink," and I realized they were probably right.

Dalton, my mother's brother, had been born when Grandma was forty. No one had to tell him he was an accident, and he seemed to live his life as if he were making up for this, rarely troubling others for attention or favors. He was self-sufficient, like Grandma, and the two of them got along easily, with an instinctual appreciation for the other's low expectations. Dalton was in high school and had his own room filled with cat skulls, dressmaking mannequins, and stuffed game. When you sat on his bed, a radio turned on. All Dalton's shirts were soft and frayed and reminded me of pajama tops, while on the bottom he always wore Wrangler jeans. If he ever gave you anything from his room, you treasured it, even if it was just an old Andy Capp comic he no longer found funny. All of Dalton's things seemed valuable because they had been kept long enough to give off his musk.

Cliff and I shared a room with Grandma across the hall, while Grandpa slept downstairs in a niche off the living room. The reason given was that he snored, and I believed it. On those cold nights when Tensie slept in the kitchen, I imagined he and Grandpa yearned for each other, regretting the forbidden territory that lay between them.

Tensie was really Dalton's dog, but Grandpa had stolen him away with heated dinners of Purina mixed with leftovers from the fridge. Sometimes they held contests beneath the dome of the huge weeping willow beside the barn, standing several feet apart and each calling Tensie's name to see who he would run to. More often than not, the dog simply lay down beside the tree's massive trunk, whimpering. "You see that?" Grandpa told Dalton. "He doesn't want to hurt your feelings," to which Dalton would reply, "He's probably just scared you'll whup him."

This idea was not so outlandish. Often Grandpa and Dalton fought, and the worst of these arguments culminated in the removal of Grandpa's belt and the lashing of Dalton's back and legs. Grandma would get between the two of them, trying to defend Dalton, then come away bruised herself. He never hit me or Cliff, though it seemed we were occasionally deserving of this, and even though he hit Dalton, whom we loved most of all, we continued to love Grandpa, too.

After Grandpa hit him, Dalton went to his room and cried. Grandpa went to the cellar, which involved stepping out onto the back porch, then descending two concrete sets of stairs that led to a wooden door. Once there, he donned a coal miner's light and sorted old nails by size into jelly jars. Back in the house, Tensie, who ultimately remained loyal to the one who had brought him to Grandpa, howled in the kitchen for as long as Dalton's sobs filtered down from the second floor. Grandma never cried. She sat at the kitchen table balancing her checkbook, which always matched her bank statement to the penny.

Grandpa used to drink, and now that he didn't, Grandma and Dalton were pretty mad at him. They were mad about a time before I was even born, when the three of them lived together in the same house where Mom lived now, in the city. The house had a long driveway, and it was Dalton's job to shovel it in winter, earning him five dollars a week. One night, when Grandpa came home from the bar to find the snow all piled up, he hauled Dalton out of bed and made him clear it right then and there, in his pajamas. Grandma tried to stop Grandpa but he pushed her into a closet. "You know what the kicker is?" Dalton asked me.

"No," I said. "What's the kicker?"

"It had started snowing *after* I went to bed. How the hell was I supposed to know?"

We laughed and laughed about this, then reenacted the scene as it had once occurred. I played Grandma, Cliff played Dalton, and Dalton played Grandpa. When he pushed me in the closet it really hurt, but I acted like it didn't. When he grabbed Cliff and shook him, yelling about how was he going to get to work in the morning, Cliff cried like the little baby that he was.

Dalton had a lot of projects, the most important of which was his motorcycle refurbishment. It was actually more of a scooter, but out of respect for Dalton we called it a motorcycle, though sometimes Grandpa called it a moped. "At least I still have my driver's license," Dalton would say, and the belt would come off. Still, Grandpa knew everything about engines, and when they weren't fighting, he passed this information along to Dalton. "Dad," Dalton might say, "help me with this spark plug." It was the only time I ever noticed him needing someone, and I was deeply jealous that it wasn't me. Another of his projects was starting a rock band. Confidently I told him, "I'll write you a hit single," which made him laugh and say, "Sure you will." He was right. I never wrote him a thing.

Grandma and I were balancing Mom's checkbook one evening (a two-person job), when a great roar emerged from the barn, and we understood that the motorcycle was up and running. We ran out on the back porch in time to see Dalton driving it up the hill, with Grandpa on the back, hugging Dalton's ribs. "Give me a ride!" I yelled, but they couldn't hear me above the sound of the engine. "You're not riding that thing," Grandma said. "Yes, I am," I told her, and we went back in the house to call Mom and see who was right.

Grandma was right, of course, but Dalton ended up giving me a ride anyway, the next time Grandma and Grandpa went to the hardware store, their favorite place to shop.

Cliff stood crying in the drive as we pulled away, not because he wanted a ride but because he was afraid to be alone in the house. We assured him Tensie would baby-sit him but he didn't believe us.

"Hold on," Dalton told me as we whizzed down Ridge Road. He had given me his only helmet to wear and his loose yellow hair whipped into my mouth as we rode, tasting of roses. I held him as Grandpa had, around the ribs, and pressed my cheek against his spine. I was hugging him tight and he didn't even know it. He probably thought I was just scared.

As we neared the school I hoped there might be some kids on the playground to see me with Dalton, but there were none. It was a gray Thursday afternoon and they were probably all at home with their nuclear families, doing homework. "See that hill?" Dalton called back to me, pointing to the incline behind the school where we went sledding over winter break.

"Yes!" I said.

"Let's test her traction!" he hollered, then turned off Ridge Road and onto the school's circular driveway. Instead of following it around, however, he quickly hopped the curb and began driving through the playground. We passed the jungle gym, the swing set, crossed the basketball court, then slipped through a space in a row of wild hedges. From there the hill seemed to go straight up. As we lost momentum, the motorcycle slowed way down and began to strain, but when I asked Dalton if he wanted me to get off, he said, "No, no, she's tough."

"But she smells funny," I said, which was true—like she was burning from the inside—and finally Dalton had to agree.

"We'll both get off," he said. "We'll walk her up, then we'll ride her down. We'll jump all those moguls, one after the other. Just keep on going, all the way back through the hedge. You're not scared, are you? If you're scared, you can walk."

I was terrified and felt pretty sure we would crash, but taking Dalton's helmet off would have made me feel even worse. "Why should I be scared?" I said, knocking on the outside of my blue fiberglass head. "I'm protected."

After pushing the motorcycle to the top of the hill, we accelerated purposefully into each mound of earth that faced us on the way down. From there we would go briefly into the air, where Dalton held the handlebars steady, maintained balance, and refused to panic as we skid-landed on the wet grass below. When we got to the bottom and passed back through the hedges, I prayed that he would not want to do this again, and he didn't. We kept riding, past the playground, then, forgoing the school's driveway altogether this time, on through the grass toward Ridge Road. Dalton was probably only concerned with hills at that point, which may have been why we wiped out in a ditch.

"I thought I could jump it," he said, a few seconds later, getting up off the ground. He had been thrown clear of the bike while my left leg was pinned underneath. There was a pasture bordering the school, and the cows grazing in it were now slowly making their way toward me, probably to sniff my head. I worried that they might also lick me, and that their animal breath would be terrifying—Tensie's times ten. "Get this thing off of me!" I shouted.

"Okay, okay," Dalton said, heaving it up by the handle-bars. He put the kickstand down, then stood above me with his hands on his hips. I noticed a tear in the right leg of his jeans. "Can you walk?" he asked me.

It hurt like hell from my knee down, but I thought I probably could. "Just help me up," I said.

He nodded and held out both hands, neither of which I took. Somehow, it didn't seem like the right approach. "Wait," he said, and he got behind me and pulled me up from under the armpits. "Can you walk?" he said again, and I took a deep breath and showed him that I could.

"Let's see if she still starts," I said, and she did.

When we got back to the house, Cliff was still in the drive with Tensie. "What took you so long?" he asked us.

We ignored him and his eyes got pretty big as he watched Dalton help me off the bike, then carry me into the house. "Don't you dare tell Mom and Dad," Dalton warned him after he had set me on the divan.

"Okay," Cliff said. "I won't tell Mom and Dad."

"*My* mom and dad," Dalton clarified. You had to do this with Cliff, as he was vengeful. When he was really mad, he had a tendency to take everything a person said at face value, then later repeat your exact instructions back to you in his own defense. It was a brilliant strategy, and I might have been more impressed had he not been such a baby.

Dalton changed his torn jeans; then we all watched *Flipper*. We let Tensie come in the living room with us and he got so excited he peed on Grandpa's recliner. Luckily it was vinyl so it wiped off pretty easily. It smelled a little but Dalton said Grandpa wouldn't notice since the alcohol had killed off his taste buds. "I smoke pot in the cellar all the time and he never says a word."

"I thought that was your perfume," I said.

Dalton laughed. "Perfume?"

"I mean cologne," I said. "Don't laugh at me."

He stopped immediately. "How's your leg?" he asked.

"Fine," I said, even though it hurt like the devil. "Maybe get me some blackberry brandy," I added. That was what Grandma gave me when I got my stomachaches after Mom's visits. She hid it upstairs, inside a roomy pump misshapen by her bunion, so Grandpa wouldn't find it. He didn't like going in Grandma's bedroom because she left the windows open year-round, creating what he called "the permafrost."

Dalton got me the brandy and it really helped. When Grandma and Grandpa came home, they asked what we had done while they were away, and we all agreed that Dalton and I had taunted Cliff from the barn loft, and that Cliff, who was too afraid to climb the ladder, had bawled his eyes out down below. "I ought to take off my belt right now," Grandpa told Dalton halfheartedly, but he didn't. Instead he gave Dalton a present, an old pair of riding goggles he had found in a thrift store at the plaza. Dalton let Cliff wear them for the rest of the night to bribe him to shut up.

At nine o'clock, Dalton picked me up and announced he was going to carry me to my room to build his strength for wrestling tryouts. First he carried me to the bathroom, where he waited outside so I could pee and brush my teeth, and then he carried me upstairs. "Your leg all right?" he asked as he set me on my bed.

"Yes," I said, reaching for the frayed cuff of his checked shirt. No one loved Dalton more than I did, and I prayed to God that night as I did every night that he would never get a girlfriend.

When Grandma came upstairs to give me a tight tuck and a kiss, she said, "Are you drunk?"

"A little," I confessed.

"Blackberry Girl," she said, which was what she called me when she felt sorry for me, "did you get a stomachache?"

I nodded.

"Did your mother call while I was out?"

"No," I said. "But I was thinking about her."

"Well, then don't think about her, for godssakes," Grandma said, and I promised I wouldn't.

In the morning my entire left leg had swelled and I couldn't get out of bed. "Shit," Dalton said when I called him into my room. "Shit shit shit!"

"Breakfast now, dammit!" Grandma yelled from the kitchen.

Dalton tried to pick me up and carry me down but I couldn't help it, I screamed. Cliff was standing by, already dressed for school. "Don't you say a fucking word!" Dalton hissed at him as he set me back down, because we could hear Grandma coming up the stairs.

"Why aren't you dressed, Patty?" she said when she got there. "Get out, Dalton! There's girls in here!"

Dalton left the room but I knew he was just outside the doorway, since I didn't hear him creaking down the steep, narrow staircase. "Grandma," I said, "I didn't tell you, but when I was climbing up to the loft I fell off the ladder and hurt my leg. I thought it would be okay by now but it really hurts and I can't walk. Sorry, Grandma."

Cliff was watching all this and I waited for him to spill the beans but he didn't.

"Why didn't you tell me?" Grandma asked. "I'm responsible for you two. Your mother has entrusted you to me. What's the matter with you?"

"I thought I would be fine," I said.

"Dalton didn't push you?"

"No!"

"I see," Grandma said. She was thinking it all over.

"I didn't push her!" Dalton said from the hallway.

"Breakfast!" Grandma yelled back at him, and he finally went downstairs.

"Let's call Mom," I said.

"After we go to the doctor's," Grandma said. Then she hollered, "Gauge! Come carry Patty downstairs. She can't walk!"

Grandpa ran up the stairs, which was hard for him to do from all his smoking, I knew, and it made me love him almost more than Dalton. "What happened here?" he asked, and Grandma told him about the loft. She told him an even more detailed story than I had told her, about how Dalton had tried to catch me when I fell and that he had gotten hurt too, but not as badly as I had. I almost interrupted then and said no, that Dalton had gone up first (which was usually the case), not me, but then I remembered it had never even happened at all.

Grandpa carried me downstairs and out to the car, with Dalton and Cliff running behind us. Grandma got her purse and keys and met us in the drive. "You sure you don't need to go to the doctor, too, son?" Grandpa asked Dalton, and he shook his head no.

"I need to go," Cliff piped up, and we all looked at him.

"Just kidding," Cliff said, and we ignored him again. Cliff sighed. I mouthed the words *shut up* to him, and I was almost sure he saw.

The doctor said i had a hairline fracture in my tibia, and he put a cast on me that ran from my heel all the way up above my knee. When Mom met us back at Grandma's, she said that was what I got for teasing poor Cliff, but Grandma disagreed with her. She said it was nobody's fault since the teasing hadn't yet begun. "There was an intent to tease!" Mom argued. "Hogwash," Grandma said, probably because she had survived Grammy Sue and secretly believed Cliff needed mental toughening. He and I were in the living room at the time, poking straw from the barn down my cast to help with the itching.

As for gym class, I was exempt until at least after winter break. Meanwhile, the doctor put a rubber stump beneath my foot so I could walk without crutches. This was fine for home but I always used them at school, since the other kids enjoyed playing with them so much. Suddenly it seemed people didn't hate me anymore. Besides the crutches, this probably had something to do with the meat Dalton had painted on my cast.

Another of Dalton's projects was to become a fine artist, and frankly I thought this was the one he would most succeed at. He had a knack for painting meat. When Grandma brought it home from the supermarket he removed it from the cellophane, positioned it on a plate, and set to work behind his easel. *Still Life with Flank Steak,* one was called, or *Still Life with Duck.* They were beautiful portraits that often included fruit and colored bottles. Dalton was especially good at re-creating the marbling of a steak. The problem was that this was a lengthy process, and occasionally the meat went bad while he was working. One time Grandma cooked it anyway, which made us all sick—particularly Grandpa, who was forced to remove his belt.

For my cast, Dalton went all out. Each cut of meat—chicken legs, pork chops, London broil—was optimally arranged, almost like a puzzle whose pieces someone had laid out without actually clicking together. What was most impressive was the way he did it all from memory, sketching first with charcoal before applying his oil paints. Looking at the finished product, I often had the sense that I was seeing inside myself, and it pleased me. "I want to be a butcher," I told Mom one weekend, and she said, "Such ambition."

Then one of the boys at school, Jared, had an accident with my crutches. He was trying to walk up the slide with them when they slipped out from beneath him and he fell and bashed his skull against the slide's steel edge. The doctors had to shave his head to stitch up the gash, and when his hair began to grow back, none appeared along the line of the scar. It looked a little bit like a tiara, and some of the fourth graders began calling him "Princess." To punish me for bringing this on him with my crutches, Corbin, Jared, and Arthur took me aside at recess one day and suggested we all urinate together. To be fair, they said, since I was the only girl, they would go first. At that point they took down their pants and peed all over my cast.

"What smells?" people asked in class after recess, and they tracked the odor to me. "She peed herself!" Corbin announced, and as quickly as they had crowded around me, they all disappeared. "Do you need to go to the nurse's office?" Mrs. Walpin said, and I told her yes, though I wasn't sure how that would help.

"Did you pee yourself?" Nurse Kimmie asked me as I lay on her padded vinyl cot. "No," I said, but I could tell she thought I was lying. She called Grandma, who arrived a few minutes later with a black plastic garbage bag to tie around my leg.

"What happened?" she asked me in the car, and I told her the whole truth. She laughed so hard she had to pull over. Then suddenly she got serious. "Oh boy," she said, daubing her eyes with a tissue. "We have to think about this. Let's just think for a minute."

I thought about it as hard as I could, until Grandma finally said, "Okay," and we got back on the road. She drove me directly to the doctor, who seemed disappointed that I had not heeded his warning to keep my cast dry. "What the heck happened?" he asked Grandma, and she said, with such naturalness, "The dog peed on her. Tensie. Just lifted his leg and peed, like she was a tree or something."

The doctor laughed and turned to me. "You're kidding!" he said.

"Nope," I said, and Grandma patted me on the back for being such a sharp Blackberry Girl.

The doctor said, "Well, it's a beauty all right, with the meat and all, but it's got to come off. It's soggy."

"No!" I said, feeling more shocked by this than by Grandma's tall tale.

But she said, "Be quiet and listen to the doctor!"

He brought out a saw and cut through my cast. It looked like he was chopping meat. I cried over what he was doing to Dalton's art, and even Grandma said, "Such a shame." Afterward, one of the nurses dumped the cast into the black garbage bag Grandma had brought and took it away. The doctor let me itch myself for a while before laying on new plaster of Paris.

When we got home Grandma put pork chops on the range for dinner. They made me think of my old cast and I started crying again. "Stop that," Grandma said, handing me a tissue from her sleeve. It was still damp from when she had dried her eyes in the car, and I felt instantly comforted by the fact that I was now in sole possession of her only tears.

Cliff had spent the afternoon sorting screws by width with Grandpa and did not seem surprised to see my new cast when he came in for dinner, though Grandpa was beside himself. "Where's the meat?" he said. "The boy worked so hard on the meat!"

"Yeah, what the hell?" Dalton said, coming down from his room. He had been listening to the Steve Miller Band when Grandma and I came in and we didn't want to disturb him.

"Tensie did it," Grandma said firmly. "He did it this morning, when Patty and I were outside collecting laundry before breakfast. She didn't notice the smell until she got to school and the other kids started making fun of her. Tensie is a bad dog, but don't listen to me, Gauge! I've only been telling you for years." Then Grandma turned to Tensie, who was eating his propped-up dinner beside the stove, and said, "Bad dog!" which made him cry and run under the table.

"Dammit, Tensie!" Grandpa said. "Get out here!" But he wouldn't come. So Grandpa reached under the table and pulled him out by the collar. "Out!" Grandpa said, pulling Tensie across the pale yellow linoleum and toward the back door. "Out!" he said again.

"Easy, Dad!" Dalton said.

"Dog urine on the cast for godsakes," Grandma said, and we all sat down to dinner.

After the serving dishes had been passed around and Grandma had taken her first bite, the rest of us picked up our utensils. "Stop kicking your feet under the table," Grandpa told Cliff.

"I'm not," Cliff said.

Grandpa set down his fork and lowered his voice in the way he did to reprimand grandchildren. "Don't lie to me, son," he said. "I can see your shoulders shaking, you got it? We don't sing at the table and we don't kick our feet."

"I wasn't singing," Cliff said, although he did stop kicking.

Grandpa ignored him.

"Grandpa," Cliff said.

"What?"

"Three boys peed on Patty's cast at recess. They pulled down their pants and peed on her in a bush. I saw it."

"Now, what kind of dinner story is that?" Grandma asked him. "You want to make us all sick?"

"We don't talk like that at the table, Cliff," Grandpa said.

"But I saw it," Cliff said.

"What did you see?" Grandma asked him. "You dreary little boy!"

"Three boys peed on Patty's leg, and she let them. She told them to do it."

"I did not!" I said. "Tensie peed on me and I didn't even know! You're making us all sick!"

"Cliff," Dalton said quickly, "you want to wear my riding goggles?"

Cliff shrugged. Nobody said anything for a while. We ate our pork chops and lettuce and rutabaga and listened to Tensie cry on the porch. Then Grandpa said to Grandma, "What's he talking about?"

"Who knows," Grandma said.

"You said not to lie to you," Cliff told Grandpa. "That's what you said and I was doing what you said. I even admit I was kicking my feet under the table. I was!"

"Who wrecked your cast, Patty?" Grandpa asked me then, point-blank.

"Tensie," I said.

"You leave her out of this," Grandma said, and she stood up.

Grandpa stood up, too. He was still holding his fork and now he pointed it at Grandma, like he was going to stick it in her cheek. When he spoke, a bauble of spit landed in her hair. "You go bring that dog back inside, Rachel. I mean it. You bring him in and you give him your supper."

"Certainly," Grandma said, and she went to get Tensie, who, even though he had been crying, did not seem to want to come back in. Then Grandma picked up Grandpa's plate instead of her own and scraped it into Tensie's bowl.

Grandpa didn't wait for her to finish before he knocked her over, causing her to spill the last of his dinner onto the floor. Quickly she rolled herself into a ball, so that when Grandpa tried to give her a kick, he couldn't find a place that would hurt. Before he could try again, Dalton was up out of his chair and punching at Grandpa. Grandma unrolled herself and hopped to her feet, at which point it became difficult to tell whether she was separating Dalton from Grandpa or joining in the fight.

I punched Cliff but he just sat there, watching the three of them cry and yell and carry on. They hated each other and lied to each other, and it was probably all Grandpa's fault. I thought they were very complicated, very smart people, and I wondered if I would ever make anyone mad enough to attack me. So far the only people who hated me were the kids at school, who I didn't even like. I vowed then to find someone I could fight with—someone with a Class 4 license like Dalton's, who lived in the country and didn't mind the smell of his own shit. Together we would struggle and tussle and lie, and when it was all over, we would sit down and watch TV while the dog tested our patience from the doorway.

When Animals
Attack

"i want you to do me a favor," my mother, executive secretary, says on the telephone one Thursday.

I'm standing at my kitchen sink, washing a chicken I plan to bake for dinner. Suddenly I feel very aware of salmonella, one of my mother's archenemies, along with streptococcus and bat guano, which, studies point out, is often found on the organic produce purchased by yuppies like me and Cyrus. My mother, in turn, points the studies out to me.

"No," I say, preemptively. Her favors tend to involve me asking people she barely knows, like my in-laws or co-workers, what their favorite color or flavor is so she can buy them extravagant gifts that signify little except that she is crazy and I must be as well, since I helped her out in the first place.

"I picked up a runaway on the way to work this morning," my mother continues, "a very nice young man who needed a hundred and fifty dollars to get back to his people in Florida. He'll be arriving in Orlando at four-fifteen tomorrow and I want you to meet him at the bus station and talk to him about careers before he reboards for Tampa."

"No," I say again, removing the giblets from inside the chicken and setting them in a stainless steel bowl. "Forget it."

"And just why not?" she asks, indignant. I am a guidance counselor, which my mother seems to think is similar to being a doctor in that I am bound to help all troubled high schoolers at any time of the day or night.

"I'll be at work tomorrow at four-fifteen," I say.

"It's four-fifteen now and you're not at work," my mother argues.

I set the chicken on a plate and begin patting it dry with a paper towel. "Mom," I say, "you gave a stranger a hundred and fifty dollars?"

"He's interested in animals," she says excitedly. "That's why I thought you could encourage him to become a veterinarian. His people sound sort of, you know, common, so I thought talking with someone like you might be just the thing to set him straight."

I picture her at her desk in New Jersey: coral lipstick faded from endless coffee sipping, hair fuzzy from ineffective conditioner, locket once devoted to me and my brother (though now that mother and Farrell aren't speaking, modified to include a baby picture of Cyrus) resting atop the substantial shelf of her bosom. Over the phone I hear her boss, Dr. Mondo, dean of communications, hacking away with emphysema. He and my mother behave as if they're married, though Dr. Mondo is already married to someone else and my mother swore off men after my father left her years ago for a woman much heavier than she. This, my mother announced, was a personal affront, since at least if he was going to dump her he might have done so in a way that indicated her appearance was at fault, and not her company. It was the shame of this, she insisted, that caused her to lose face with all her girlfriends, while Farrell, fed up with her teary midnight phone calls, assured her that no, her lousy personality had simply struck again. Hence the loss of his locket ranking.

"So you'll go?" my mother asks me.

"No!" I say, resting my hand atop my own human shelf, a belly six months pregnant with a girl Cyrus wants to call Georgiette. My mother has informed him that this is unacceptable, however, and that my suggestion of Twyla is even worse. I understand she will settle for nothing less than Meredith, her own name, which has compelled Cyrus and me to refer to the baby by her chromosomal construction: Double X.

"Oh, don't be so uncharitable!" my mother says.

"Listen to your mother!" Dr. Mondo yells in the background.

"How is it that my idea of common sense equals your idea of being uncharitable?" I ask.

"Who knows what kind of crappy ideals you picked up in college?" my mother says, irritated, while Dr. Mondo chuckles nearby. "In any case," she continues, her voice alarmingly smooth, "it turns out you *have* to go and meet the boy."

"Why?" I say.

"Because he has something for you."

"What?" In my head, I quickly compose a list of things I'd be happy to do without: money, baby clothes, a dozen real bagels.

"Your baby pictures," my mother says. "Didn't you ask me for those?"

I did indeed. I am a pregnant, thirty-four-year-old guidance counselor who recently had a hankering for my baby pictures and expressed as much to my mother, who in turn expressed a reluctance to send them through the mail as there are no remaining negatives, and the post office is completely incompetent.

I wash my hands with orange antibacterial soap, then move down the counter to a spot where we keep Post-it notes and a cup of pens. "Okay, Mom," I say. "Tell me again what time he gets in?"

She repeats the boy's itinerary and I do not bother to point out he probably won't be on the bus, and that she and I will never see my three-month-old bare butt being washed in her kitchen sink again.

We hang up. I return to the chicken and rub its skin with

olive oil, salt, pepper, and garlic. Cyrus will be home shortly, and when he sees I have made dinner he will kiss me everywhere and tell me how wonderful it is to have the night off from cooking. He will then tell me I most certainly will not meet a runaway at the Greyhound station tomorrow, after which I will tell him about the baby pictures, and he will curse my mother and the biology lecture he cannot afford to cancel the following afternoon. He will want to call my brother, Farrell, instead, who lives nearby, but I will assure him that the bus station is a public place and I will be perfectly safe. After much hemming and hawing he will concede that I am a grown woman who knows how to take care of herself, though if anything happens to me or Double X, he swears, it will be curtains for Meredith.

The next day i chicken out and call Farrell myself. He is only in Orlando temporarily, studying storm trends for the National Weather Service in the city with the greatest number of lightning strikes per year. Farrell himself was struck by lightning as a teenager one April morning. He had just screamed at my mother for telling me and my father he must have had a wet dream since why else would he be washing his own sheets before breakfast, then stormed out of the house, threatening never to return. Eyewitnesses saw him pedaling maniacal figure eights in the relatively empty high school parking lot (it was a Saturday) when a storm rolled in and he was knocked to the ground by a crinkly yellow bolt. Doctors attributed his survival to his great physical strength (he was a varsity linebacker) and the fact that the rubber tires on his ten-speed were poor conductors of electricity. Still, he was no longer able to play football after the accident, and his memory was short-circuited. Though he remained hateful toward my mother, he could not recall specifically why, much to her delight. She made my father and me promise not to remind him of the wet-dream argument, and I agreed, not for her sake but because I didn't want to embarrass Farrell a second time. My mother then threw away his old sheets and made his bed up with brand-new ones. When Farrell returned from the hospital and asked where she had bought them, she shook her head sadly at what had become of her son's mind, then gently reminded him we'd had these since he was a kid.

Because he heads his Orlando research team, I know Farrell can get time off at the last minute, especially with the safety of his beloved niece at issue. This is the reason I tell myself I am calling him, in any case. The fact that he can get particularly violent where my mother and her shenanigans are concerned is neither here nor there. Double X requires protection, no matter the cost. Anyone would agree with me on this.

"That stupid bitch!" Farrell yells when I get him on the phone. It is 3:30 in the afternoon and I have just seen my last appointment of the day, an Indian senior in tears over a postgraduate arranged marriage her parents are planning for her. Nothing makes me feel more powerless than other people's cultures. If only she had been pregnant or abusing drugs I might have been of some real help.

"Don't say 'bitch,' Farrell," I say wearily.

"Why not?" he asks.

"It's very antiwoman," I instruct him. "There's no equally derogatory term for men, so until there is, we have to be fair." This works well with my male students in that it seems to give them a bizarre hope for the future. Farrell, too, has heard it before, but the lightning keeps him from retaining it.

"Oh right," he says. "I forgot."

"That's okay," I say.

"But she is such a stupid cow! I mean, picking up boys on the highway and giving them money just because they ask for it? Pleased to meet ya, shit for brains!"

"Be that as it may," I say, "I've agreed to meet this kid at the bus station and I really don't feel like going alone."

"I don't know, Joyce. There's a big storm coming in."

"C'mon, Farrell," I say. "For the baby."

He sighs. "As long as I'm back at the weather station before the storm."

"What time does it start?" I ask him.

"Say, oh, seven thirty-eight P.M." Farrell is the only person I know who expects the weather like a favored dinner guest: nervously and with high hopes for a glorious evening.

"We should be done by then."

"Did she send any of *my* baby pictures along?" he asks.

"I don't know. I mean, I'm sure you're probably in some of mine."

"Unless she cut me out."

"I doubt it, Farrell."

"Stupid bitch."

"Farrell!"

"What?" he asks sincerely.

"Never mind," I say.

In the outer office my secretary, Gwynn, is eating from a box of chocolates my mother sent her the previous week. "Want one?" she asks as I head out the door.

"No thanks," I say.

"Why did your mother send these again?" she says. "Refresh my memory."

Gwynn likes a good laugh, and I decide to humor her. "Because," I say, trying to recall my mother's exact words, "she's so glad that you, unlike so many other secretaries, know your place and do not feel resentful toward me simply because I am your boss."

"What if I increase my words per minute? What do I get for that?"

"Job satisfaction," I say.

Gwynn laughs again and calls me a bitch, which I permit her to do on occasion, and we say good night.

In the car on the way to the bus station I can see Farrell's storm approaching—a series of gray, smoking clouds ruining a vacationer's sky. They remind me of Farrell himself and the doom he brought to our family after the accident. For he became increasingly angry at my mother as the years went by, who cried pitifully in response and demanded to know what she had done but nurse him back to health, after all? "You know what you've done!" he would tell her uncertainly, and we would all give a start because it was true, she did. I decided if Farrell ever asked me about that Saturday in April I would immediately tell him the truth, but he never did, and I couldn't bring myself to raise the issue of the wet dream first. It was part embarrassment, part selfishness on my part, as I had come to relish his attacks on my mother. In his rage he spoke for both of us. Often I pictured myself as hysterical as Farrell, screaming at Meredith, her fleshy neck caught between my hands, but I had not been struck by lightning and so had no excuse.

The Greyhound station is one of those modern-looking brick structures that seems like it could be worn as a helmet should someone decide to shrink it down. As I pull into the parking lot I see that Farrell is already there, idling the engine of his black truck. His vanity license plate from New Jersey reads LIT-NIN, while painted along each side of the truck are jagged renderings of the bolts that once struck him.

When he sees me coming, Farrell cuts his engine and eases out of the truck, briefly checking the sky, as is his habit. He remains a big man but he moves slowly and painfully, as if the electricity were still in his bones, shocking him. Only his eyes move quickly anymore, alert to the slightest atmospheric change. His standard uniform is jeans and sneakers along with a neatly pressed shirt, and as he comes toward me, I take in the familiar smell of English Leather.

"Hey, Double X," he says, throwing a genial, fake punch at my stomach, something that never fails to set Cyrus on edge. "Hey, Joyce."

We hug lazily, then head toward the station entrance. "What's this guy's name anyway?" Farrell asks as he opens the front door for me.

"Ellsworth," I say mournfully.

"Ellsworth!" he yells, and several people inside turn to look at us. "That's not a real name."

"Quiet down, Farrell," I say, looking around the station. To our left is the ticket counter; the waiting area takes up the central part of the building directly in front of us, with all its molded plastic chairs and requisite pay-TVs. To our right is an impressive bank of vending machines and, looming in the distance for those requiring a meal, a small kitchen offers made-to-order hamburgers. The place smells of smoke (though there are No Smoking signs everywhere), and is mostly populated by unkempt teenagers hauling backpacks and tired women hauling children.

"Is that where he comes in?" Farrell asks, pointing to the set of doors along the glass wall bordering the waiting area.

I nod. Each door leads outside to one of several diagonal parking bays, where already two buses rest, chugging gas so the passengers aboard can enjoy some air-conditioning in the offensive May heat. "That one," I say, pointing to empty Bay 6.

Farrell nods and checks his watch. "We have a few minutes. You hungry?"

"I'm always hungry, Farrell," I say, laying a hand on the baby.

We trek over to the counter and order two burgers each, along with french fries and soft drinks. "Make sure they're well done, now," Farrell tells the young woman cooking our food. "We've got a pregnant lady here."

She nods fearfully as she pulls on her food-service gloves. Inside them her fingernails are long and pink, while under her hair net I sense a meticulously styled 'do just waiting to escape. "Don't say things like that to young people, Farrell," I tell him. "You'll frighten them."

"Ever heard of *E. coli?*" he counters. "You'll thank me when you don't have the shits tonight." He persists in keeping an eye on the food preparation, while I keep an eye on him, watching for signs of the red face or sweaty temples that indicate his internal rage is not far from the surface. Aside from the tense muscles in his neck, however, he's clean.

Farrell insists on paying, after which we sit down with our meals, squeezing plastic pouches of ketchup and mustard indiscriminately over everything. "So what do we do when he gets here?" Farrell asks, eating roughly one-third of his burger in the first bite.

"*If* he's on the bus," I say, licking grease from my fingers, "I plan to get my pictures and leave."

Farrell affects a warbly falsetto meant to be an imitation of my mother. "You mean you're not going to counsel him about careers?"

I laugh and pop a fry into my mouth. "I don't think so."

"Here's the thing," Farrell says. "I'm already here. I've got some time."

"So?" I say.

"Maybe I'll counsel him."

"About what?"

"Careers. I'm an accomplished meteorologist. I have a lot to offer a kid."

"We'll just get the pictures and leave," I say.

"We'll get the pictures and see what happens. Leave our options open." He shoves the last of his second burger in his mouth, then reaches for my second burger, which I have not yet started. "Can I have this?" he asks, and I nod.

"He probably won't even be on the bus," I say, and suddenly I feel tears coming to my eyes. "My baby pictures are probably lying in a ditch somewhere on the Jersey Turnpike."

"What does this kid look like anyway?"

"Mom says he's rail-thin and wears a jean jacket. She thinks he seems a little bit gay."

"What the hell does that mean?" Farrell says.

I sigh. "She says his hair is shiny and clean and he seems to know a lot about hair-care products."

"That stereotypical bitch."

"I really wish you would stop saying that."

"What?"

"Bitch."

"Why?"

"It's offensive. It offends me. What if someone called me or Double X a bitch? How would you like that?"

"But they wouldn't call you that."

"Sure they would."

"Not in front of me. They'd be too scared."

"So as long as you don't know about it, it's all right?"

"Joyce," he says plaintively, "that's the only word I have to describe Mom. I don't know any other words."

He looks slightly panicked and I decide to lay off him. We load up all the trash on our orange plastic trays, dump it, then go stand in front of Bay 6, where the bus from Jacksonville is just pulling in, and a young man with shiny black hair is the first person to descend the Greyhound's grooved, metal steps.

"mrs. marquette!" Ellsworth yells as he bursts through the glass door and into the bus station. I assume my mother has told him of my pregnancy and that this is how he is able to identify me so quickly. "I'm so pleased to finally meet you," he says now, coming toward me with an outstretched hand. I'm momentarily surprised, as none of the kids I counsel seem to have been taught this simple gesture by their parents. I take Ellsworth's hand and shake it, and as soon as we're finished, he reaches into a tote bag reading I LOVE NY and whips out the album containing my baby pictures. "First of all," he says, his breath a sweet mixture of chocolate and pot, "let me give you this. I'm sure you've been pretty worried about it. I told your mother not to give it to me just in case anything happened, but she said she trusted me like a son, so here you go!"

"She said what?" Farrell says. He's beginning to go a little bit red now, and I understand that soon I will not be able to make him hear me on any subject.

"Ellsworth," I say, tucking the photo album under my arm, "this is my brother, Farrell."

"Oh," Ellsworth says, and his face drops a little, which tells me my mother has been very busy indeed. Still, he holds out his hand and says, "Pleased to meet you, sir."

Farrell takes Ellsworth's hand and squeezes it hard, so that after they let go, Ellsworth places the hand behind his back, as if hiding it might erase his discomfort. "So she trusts you like a son, eh? Well, I hate to tell you, Ellsworth, but that's not a compliment."

"Yes sir," Ellsworth says, nodding.

"What kind of manners are those, anyway?" Farrell asks him. "I thought runaways didn't have manners."

"It's just that my dad's in the air force, so that's where I learned it, I guess."

Farrell nods. "You going back to your family in Tampa?"

"Yes sir," Ellsworth says. "I had a long talk with your mother and she really thinks it's what's best for me."

Farrell and I stare at him blankly. We are unaware of anyone who might follow Meredith's advice. Ellsworth smiles then, revealing charmingly crooked teeth that have clearly never seen braces, and frankly don't need to. Next he removes the stuffed red backpack from his shoulders and sets it on the floor beside his tote bag. In the face of our silence he finally blurts out, "Mrs. Marquette, your mother is so sweet! You must love her."

"That's a little strong, isn't it?" Farrell asks, agitated, but Ellsworth's eyes are glued to me, waiting for my response.

"Somewhat," I say numbly. Try as I might, I feel incapable of putting this young man at ease or shielding him from my brother, who I can see is gearing up for something. If only we were back in my office at school, the one with the sign on the door saying my name and that I am a guidance counselor, I might know what to do. If only my secretary were here.

"She loves you, I know that," Ellsworth says.

"What about me?" Farrell demands.

"Oh sure," Ellsworth says, nodding eagerly at Farrell. "Anyway," he says, "I was wondering if I could buy you guys some dinner and maybe talk a little bit about colleges with you, Mrs. Marquette. I really want to get my life back on track, you know?"

"Just for the record," Farrell says, "who exactly is paying for this dinner?"

Ellsworth looks at Farrell, then at me, then back at Farrell. "Okay, I mean, sure, that's a good point. Because I guess your mom told you she really helped me out a lot financially, and so that's true, actually. Yeah. Technically she's the one buying the dinner."

Farrell nods.

"Of course, in the end I'll be the one paying since I'm going to pay her back every penny. That was all I meant, I guess. About me paying."

"Good man," Farrell says, clapping Ellsworth on the back. "Tell it like it is!" He then picks up the boy's luggage for him and we all head back to the restaurant counter, where Farrell and I each order two hot dogs. The girl behind the counter smiles at me and we say hi. Her name tag reads CLARICE.

Ellsworth pays for the food as promised and leads us back to our old table, where Clarice has not yet wiped up the stray gobs of ketchup and mustard from our previous meal. "God," Ellsworth says, using his own napkin to clean up some of the mess, "people eat like pigs!"

Behind his back, Farrell and I look at each other. My brother smiles at me serenely, for Ellsworth has just given him a gift, a reason to attack. Since he was struck by lightning I have come to imagine Farrell's brain as a complex series of wires instead of blood vessels, and now they are telegraphing a message to me: *Did you hear that? He just called us pigs!* No matter that Farrell and I really do eat like pigs. What's important now is that Ellsworth understand that the affection he shares with our mother does not make him our brother. Regrettably and quite involuntarily, I offer Farrell a wink.

We sit down. Farrell engages aggressively with his condiment packets. "Anyway, Mrs. Marquette," Ellsworth says, trying not to look as the ketchup and mustard begin to flow, "I was telling your mother how much I like animals, and that was when she suggested I become a veterinarian."

I wipe some of Farrell's ketchup off my drink cup and nod.

"Oh, hold on," Farrell says, reaching into his pocket for

a pen. He takes a napkin and writes VETERINARIAN at the top of it, then PROS and CONS beneath that, drawing a line between the two words to create columns.

"Oh," Ellsworth says, watching him.

"What a good idea, Farrell," I add, willing Ellsworth to believe I mean this.

Farrell says, "It's a little trick I use to help keep my brain straight." He looks at Ellsworth then and taps the side of his head. "You know, short-term memory loss and all."

Ellsworth clears his throat. "From when you were struck by lightning, sir?"

Farrell nods.

"May I ask what that felt like, sir?"

"Like fucking a rosebush," Farrell says.

Ellsworth nods slowly, then takes a sip of his Coke. "Do you know anything about veterinarians, Mrs. Marquette?" he asks me after his drink goes down.

I find myself saying, "Just because you like animals doesn't mean you should be a veterinarian."

"Oh," he says. "I guess I never thought of it that way."

"How do you feel about blood and fecal matter?" Farrell says. "Because that's what it's really about, you know. It's a mess."

"Hmm," Ellsworth says.

"Same with childbirth," I tell him. "Everyone says it's so beautiful but it's not. It's gross. I might even crap myself in the process."

"Oh boy," Ellsworth says.

"It's not like working in a petting zoo, for godssakes!" Farrell puts in.

"No," Ellsworth says, "I mean, I didn't think it would be. Of course, even as a vet, you would have to pet the animals sometimes, right? To put them at ease?"

"I suppose so," I say.

"One thing I was thinking," Farrell begins slowly, "is about your hair. You have lovely, shiny hair, Ellsworth."

Ellsworth touches his hair with his hand. "Thank you."

"Did you notice my mother's hair?" I ask him.

He shakes his head.

"She uses generic conditioner. That's why it's so frizzy. She's kind of cheap."

"Really? Hmm. I mean, I guess I thought she was pretty generous with me."

"I object!" Farrell announces abruptly, standing up from the table. He walks over to the vending machines and begins pacing in front of them. His thin, curly hair has gotten a little wild looking, though I don't recall having seen him run his hands through it.

Ellsworth leans across the table toward me now. "Is he all right, Mrs. Marquette? I mean, I don't mean to be rude, but your mother says he's crazy. She says she had to remove his picture from her locket because it was too painful to look at him anymore, the way he used to be."

"Here's the thing," I say sympathetically. "I think all my brother is trying to say is, have you considered the field of hairdressing?"

"Pardon me?" Ellsworth says.

"You just strike both of us as more of a hairdresser than a veterinarian. Do you enjoy that sort of thing?"

"Well," Ellsworth says, retreating back into his seat. "I mostly just like animals, I guess. I thought you might have some advice for me since your mom said you were a guidance counselor."

Just then Farrell returns with packages of Oreos for each of us. "He doesn't want to be a hairdresser," I say.

"But why!" Farrell yells. Several people in the waiting area turn to look at us, and Farrell acknowledges them by announcing, "This boy is a runaway who has finally come home!" The people see it is not wise to get involved, even if this is true, and they look away.

Ellsworth stands up then. "I'm afraid I'm imposing on both of you," he says shakily. "I'm going back to Tampa to enroll in community college. I promise I'll do lots of research on what it really means to be a veterinarian, taking into account what you've said here today. Thank you very much for your help."

With that he picks up his bags and heads over to a chair with a coin-operated TV attached. Farrell and I watch as he takes several deep breaths, then puts a quarter in the slot and begins watching *Oprah*.

"Let's get out of here," I say to Farrell. He nods, and before we know it, we're in TV chairs, too, on either side of Ellsworth.

"Hi, Ellsworth," Farrell says.

"Hi," Ellsworth says.

"We're going to leave soon," I assure him. "My husband, Cyrus, and I have a ballroom-dancing class tonight and Farrell is tracking a storm."

Ellsworth nods politely.

"Watcha watchin'?" Farrell asks.

"This is *The Oprah Winfrey Show*," Ellsworth says.

Farrell nods. He offers Ellsworth the PROS and CONS napkin he created earlier, except now the word VETERINARIAN has been crossed out and replaced with HAIRDRESSER. "You can keep this if you like," Farrell says. "It might help you to make up your mind later on."

Ellsworth takes the napkin, reads it, then places it inside his jean jacket.

"Ellsworth," I say, trying to sound sincere, "I'm sorry I couldn't be of more help."

He nods again, keeping his eyes on the TV and Oprah's special guest, a child who is meeting his long-lost father for the first time.

"Do you have any other career-related questions?" I ask him.

He shakes his head so that the black shiny hair catches the fluorescent lights above and nearly glitters. On the other side of him, Farrell can't seem to resist as he reaches out to stroke the boy's head. A couple of tears spill from Ellsworth's eyes, though he refuses the tissue I offer him.

Suddenly Farrell stands up. "Bon voyage, kiddo!" he says, then turns and walks away. We both watch him lope out of the station. For a second I think about following him, but then we'd have to talk to each other and I'm not sure what we'd say. Anyway, my work now is with Ellsworth—cleaning up the mess my family and I have made of his juvenile life.

In the end he decides to take my tissue. "This wasn't even my idea," he says. "I was going to stay in New York and try to get a job until your mother gave me those stupid pictures. She said I would ruin my mother's life if I didn't go home. She doesn't even know my mother!"

I nod.

"I didn't have to do this, you know!"

I hand him another tissue. He tells me a little about his family in Tampa and, to his surprise, I counsel him not to go back there. I charge him a ticket to New York instead, then give him all the cash in my wallet, a little over eighty dollars. I instruct him to stay away from my mother and not to ride his bicycle in the rain, if he ever gets one. Everything I say seems to make sense to him. When his bus pulls away at 7:00 P.M., he smiles at me and waves, while I imagine him sleeping in a cardboard box beneath the Brooklyn Bridge.

Outside in the parking lot, Farrell's truck is long gone, while his storm is rollicking overhead. It will follow me home, briefly threaten my safety and sense of well-being, then move on to harass someone else. Meanwhile, Cyrus and I will dance the fox-trot to the Abba music our instructor likes to play, and I will tell him a modified version of what happened at the bus station—one that doesn't make me and Farrell look quite so bad. I will tell him I can't wait for Double X to be born because I just have this feeling I'm going to be a great mother. Three months later, when she finally does appear and I scan her eyes for any memory of my transgressions, I will see only hunger and rage.